Jean E Foster
4 th Set
Nov 1993

# Forever  Romances

# In Name Only

Irene Hannon

## Forever 🌹 Romances

is an imprint of
Guideposts Associates, Inc.
Carmel, NY 10512

To my wonderful parents,
who taught me the meaning of love.

This Guideposts edition is published by special arrangement with Thomas Nelson Communications.

Printed in the United States of America.

Scripture quotations are from the Revised Standard Version of the Bible, copyrighted 1946, 1952, © 1971, 1973.

ISBN 0-8407-7363-3

*Chapter One*

Brooke Peyton slowly sipped a tall, frosty glass of lemonade and gazed about her in delight. The gaily striped umbrella tilted jauntily over her tiny table at a sidewalk café in Nice. She sighed contentedly, enjoying the view of the sparkling Mediterranean and speculating about the lives of the people who were passing along the beach between her and the azure sea.

Were any of those suntanned men with the dark good looks among the ranks of the playboys who, she had heard, occupied this resort? A smile played at her generous lips, revealing rows of even white teeth. Then she chided herself for being so fanciful. At least no one could accuse her of being unimaginative!

She still found it hard to believe that she was actually on the French Riviera, but it was true. Her eyes danced with delight as she told herself again how fortunate she was to have this chance to travel in Europe. It was a dream come true, and she owed it all to Elizabeth Bates.

Brooke rested her chin in a small hand that was graced with tapering fingers as she traveled back in her memory. Her deep brown eyes, with their entrancing amber flecks, grew thoughtful. The long waves of her russet-colored hair glistened like burnished copper as the sun danced across them, and a capricious breeze

5

lifted them to reveal the perfect oval of her face and its porcelain-like complexion.

Her casual attire of blue jeans and a knit top made her look much younger than her twenty-six years, but it did not conceal her innate femininity.

Brooke was accustomed to the second looks and comments that inevitably came with her unusual combination of dark brown eyes and reddish hair. But at the moment she was unaware of the admiring glances directed toward her. She was conscious only of a warm, grateful glow as she recalled the events of the last year and the benefactress who had made this trip possible.

The first thing Brooke had noticed when she met Elizabeth Bates the year before was the woman's vitality. Her zest for life was clearly revealed in her direct, interested gaze, her open manner, and the laugh lines around her eyes. Had her gray hair not betrayed her age, Brooke would have guessed her to be about forty.

Later, Brooke had discovered that the woman was nearing her sixty-fifth birthday, a fact that bore out one of Brooke's long-held beliefs: chronological age is only one—and certainly not the most important—measure of age. In spirit, Elizabeth Bates would always remain a young woman.

Mrs. Bates had come into the exclusive clothing shop in London where Brooke worked, and as her usual saleswoman was on vacation, Brooke had been assigned to help her. Carolyn Evans, the manager, had drawn Brooke aside and warned her that Mrs. Bates was a bit of an eccentric.

Brooke, who had been working at the shop for only a few weeks, had been a bit nervous as Carolyn drew her toward the short, slightly stocky woman. *Eccentric* could mean a lot of things, and Brooke had just barely grown accustomed to dealing with the rather reserved people who frequented the exclusive shop. But the merry twinkle in the older woman's eyes put her at ease from the moment they were introduced. Brooke well remembered their first conversation.

"You're an American, aren't you?" Mrs. Bates had said. "Are you a student?"

"I was. I finished my graduate studies in May, and now I'm working to save enough money to go back to the United States."

"Lovely country," the woman commented. "I enjoy the East Coast, but I don't think there's any better skiing in the world than in Colorado. Of course, it's becoming a bit crowded now. Pity. When I was there last year I had to wait in the lift line for forty-five minutes." She looked up and caught Brooke's expression of incredulity. "Is something wrong, my dear?" she asked innocently, her eyes twinkling.

"Of course not," Brooke said, recovering quickly. "It's just that, well..." Her voice trailed off, and a bright red flush appeared on her cheeks. Mrs. Bates chuckled and finished the thought for her.

"You didn't expect someone my age to be interested in skiing. No, no, that's quite all right. I must admit I don't look the type. That's one of the sad things about growing old, you know. Inside, you feel the same as you did at twenty-five, and every time you look in the mirror you are shocked by the face that stares back at you. But Father Time is not going to stop me from doing the things I want to do," she finished, with an impish wink at Brooke.

Brooke was captivated. If eccentric meant enjoying life to the fullest, then Elizabeth Bates was one of the most eccentric people she had ever met. Despite their difference in age, Brooke sensed a kindred spirit. It was apparently a mutual perception, for on subsequent visits to the shop Mrs. Bates had always requested Brooke's assistance.

Mrs. Bates traveled extensively, and Brooke always looked forward to hearing stories of her various adventures. There seemed to be nothing she hadn't tried, from riding a camel in Egypt to traveling down the Amazon in a dugout canoe.

Although Brooke considered her own life dull in comparison, Mrs. Bates nevertheless seemed genuinely interested in it, and Brooke found herself opening up in a way she rarely did, telling her about the tragic death of her parents in a car accident three years earlier—just prior to her college graduation—and her subsequent fellowship to study abroad for an advanced history degree.

"No one could have asked for better parents than mine," she confided once as they sat drinking tea while Mrs. Bates's latest purchases were being wrapped. "They were always there when I needed them, encouraging me to do things I never dreamed I could do. Everything I am today I owe to them."

"It sounds like they were wonderful people, Brooke." Mrs. Bates took the younger woman's hand in a comforting clasp. "You must miss them terribly."

"I do." Brooke lowered her eyes, which were filled with poignant sadness. "I guess I miss them even more intensely than most people would, because I don't have any brothers or sisters, or even any relatives. I learned the real meaning of loneliness when they died. To know you'll never see someone you love again in this world…"

She stopped for a moment, her voice too choked to continue. Mrs. Bates squeezed her hand, and Brooke gave her an apologetic smile.

"Sorry. I still get this way when I talk about it. The only thing that helped me survive their death was my faith. I truly believe that I'll see Mom and Dad again someday, and that's what keeps me going. Death has just changed their life, not ended it."

"I know precisely what you mean, Brooke," Mrs. Bates said, smiling tenderly. "I believe the same thing about Roger, my husband. Ours was a marriage in the

8

fullest sense of the word. We were lovers, of course, but even more than that we were friends. The union of spirit is even more important in the long term than the union of body, my dear. Roger and I had that spiritual union. When he died so suddenly, I thought my world had ended. But even though the pain and emptiness never go away, their sharpness fades with time, Brooke. And eventually you take out all the wonderful memories that at first you put on a shelf in your heart because they are too painful to remember. And they give you a great deal of joy."

Mrs. Bates paused and smiled gently at Brooke.

"You know, I'm not a religious zealot by any means. But there is one Bible verse that always gives me comfort: 'So faith, hope, love abide, these three; but the greatest of these is love.' Roger gave me the gift of love, as your parents gave it to you, Brooke. It is the most wonderful gift with which we can be blessed, because it transcends time and death. Death is only a temporary parting."

Brooke was deeply touched by the woman's words, and she impulsively hugged Mrs. Bates.

"Thank you," she said simply. "I haven't really talked to anyone heart-to-heart since my parents died."

"They would have been most proud of all you've accomplished, Brooke, as well as of the person you are," Mrs. Bates said as she rose to take the packages a saleswoman handed her. "I'll see you soon."

"I'll look forward to it," Brooke replied warmly.

On another of Mrs. Bates's visits to the shop Brooke had mentioned her life in London and her roommate, Mary Clifford.

"It's not a permanent arrangement, though," Brooke explained as she helped Mrs. Bates select some items for her next trip—an African photo safari. "I plan to go back to the United States just as soon as I can save the airfare and enough to hold me over until I get a job— which may take awhile," she added ruefully. "People with master's degrees in history aren't in great demand, I'm afraid, even those who have studied English history at the source. It's taking me longer than I expected to save enough to return, but I'm enjoying London tremendously."

"I hope you're not planning to go home without first seeing some of the continent!" exclaimed Mrs. Bates, genuinely shocked.

"Well, I've traveled quite a bit in the British Isles, but more extensive traveling will have to wait until some future date, I think," Brooke said casually, not wishing to dwell on her meager finances. "Someday, though, I'll take the grand tour," she finished gaily.

Mrs. Bates made no further comment, and the talk turned to her upcoming trip. Brooke was almost as excited as her customer as she helped her prepare for her next adventure. Vicariously traveling to exotic places wasn't the same as going, of course, but with Mrs. Bates it could still be a lot of fun.

Fleetingly Brooke wondered what it would be like to have the money to take such trips whenever the whim arose. Probably pretty wonderful, she decided. Not many people were in Mrs. Bates's situation, though. She could afford to indulge her love of travel several times a year. But Brooke knew that she devoted most of her time and money to charitable causes, for she had no close relatives. She was a marvelous person, and Brooke felt honored that the woman seemed to enjoy her company.

"Well, I think that should be everything you'll need," Brooke said with a slight frown as she glanced at the items they'd assembled. "Africa! I bet you'll have a great time!"

"I always do," Mrs. Bates replied promptly. "If you go into a situation with a positive attitude, it's usually quite enjoyable."

"Be sure to let me hear from you when you return," Brooke reminded her. "I want a full account!"

"Just try to stop me! You're my best listener. After all, not many people want to listen to an old woman's ramblings."

"Old!" Brooke scoffed. "That's ridiculous. You're one of the youngest people I know."

The older woman smiled and patted Brooke's hand.

"Thank you, my dear. That's one of the nicest compliments I've ever had."

"Have a good trip!" Brooke said, walking her to the door. "I'll be waiting to hear all about it."

As it turned out, Brooke waited a long time—three months to be exact. At first, as the weeks went by, she wasn't too worried, but eventually, she began to feel a vague uneasiness.

Finally, Brooke had to admit that something must be wrong. She had known Mrs. Bates for almost a year, and it wasn't like her to wait so long after a trip to come into the shop. Brooke now had almost enough money saved to return to the States. But she couldn't leave without saying good-bye to Mrs. Bates, and one night, curled up on the couch in their small but cozy living room, Brooke confided her worry to Mary.

"I can't understand why she's stayed out of touch for so long," she said, drawing her long, shapely legs up and resting her chin on her knees. "I hope there's nothing wrong."

Mary, slightly plump and with a pleasant, round face, sat across from Brooke. She kicked off her shoes and put her feet on the footstool. "Why don't you just write her a note, Brooke? The store must have her address if she's a regular customer."

"I suppose I could," Brooke admitted. "But I hate to bother her if she's busy."

"Oh, pooh," Mary waved her protest aside. "From what you've told me, she's a very down-to-earth person. She'd probably love to hear from you."

"I suppose so," Brooke replied.

Despite her reluctance to intrude on Mrs. Bates at

home, she looked up the woman's address the next day at work, intending to write her that evening. As it turned out, however, a letter would have been useless. Mary met her at the door when she arrived at the tiny flat, and her usually cheery friend wore a solemn expression.

"I'm afraid I have some bad news for you, Brooke." Silently Mary handed her the evening paper, pointing to an item in the middle of the page. The headline read, "Elizabeth Bates, city benefactress, dies."

For a moment the page blurred before Brooke's eyes and the room tilted crazily, but when Mary took her arm in a firm grip the world righted itself. Gently her friend led her to the couch, and Brooke sank down, her eyes dully scanning the columns of type.

"Elizabeth Bates, 65, died Tuesday after a brief illness. Mrs. Bates became ill shortly after returning from Africa three months ago. She died at her home in London."

The story continued, listing her many charitable activities and contributions, but Brooke was too numb to comprehend all that she was reading. Instead she kept picturing Mrs. Bates as she'd last seen her, so vital and alive as she prepared for her safari. Miserably, her eyes brimming with tears, she looked over at Mary.

"I'm so sorry, love. I know how much you liked her," Mary murmured sympathetically.

"I didn't even know she was sick," Brooke protested in a choked voice, tears clouding her vision. "I would have visited her if I had."

"That's probably why she didn't tell you. Mrs. Bates didn't sound like the kind of person who would want anyone to spend time at a sickbed. And she wouldn't have wanted you to mourn, Brooke, you know that. She was too full of life to want anyone to waste time being sad when they could be enjoying life."

"I suppose you're right." Brooke nodded, but the ache in her heart remained.

For the next few days Brooke immersed herself in plans for returning to the States. She was glad she would not be working much longer, for she invariably found herself looking up whenever the door opened and experiencing a sharp pang of sorrow when she realized that Mrs. Bates would not be among those visiting the shop.

Brooke arrived home one evening during her last week at the shop to find Mary fixing dinner in the kitchen. She sniffed appreciatively. "Smells good, Mary," she called. "I'm hungry."

"That's good news. You haven't been eating much the last few days. Oh, there's a letter for you on the table in the living room. It's from a solicitor." Mary poked her head out of the tiny kitchen. "Are you in trouble with the law or something?" she asked with a mischievous grin.

"Not that I know of," Brooke replied with a smile, curiously examining the envelope. "I wonder what it is?"

"Well, there's only one way to find out." Mary stood watching in the doorway, wiping her hands on her apron.

Brooke made a face at her friend and then tore open the envelope, quickly scanning the contents.

"I don't believe it!" she said finally.

"What is it?"

"It's from Mrs. Bates's lawyer. It says I'm mentioned in her will, and I'm supposed to call for an appointment."

"You're joking!"

"No, it's true. Read it yourself." Mary took the letter and read it slowly. Then she handed it back with a grin.

"You must have made quite an impression. What do you suppose she left you?"

"I haven't the faintest idea," Brooke said in bewilderment as she read the letter through again. "But I guess I'll find out soon enough. I'll call tomorrow and make an appointment with the lawyer. It's probably just a remembrance of some sort. But I'm really touched that she cared enough to mention me in her will at all."

Two days later, sitting across from the thin, middle-aged lawyer in his office, Brooke prepared to find out what her bequest was.

"Well, Miss Peyton, you are a lucky young woman. Mrs. Bates was a most generous woman, you know, and you are on the receiving end of some of her generosity. I won't bore you with all the legal terms in the will," he said as he adjusted his wire-rimmed glasses and picked up a sheet of paper. "To put it simply, Mrs. Bates left you a sum of money that she expressly indicated should be used for travel in Europe. It's quite a generous amount."

Brooke gasped when he read the figure, and he paused to peer disapprovingly at her over the tops of his glasses. "It should allow you to take a very nice trip," he finished, consulting the paper in front of him. "There is one section I'd like to read to you, and of course I'll give you a copy to take with you." He cleared his throat and began to read.

Brooke has been my traveling companion—in memory—on many occasions, and this is my way of thanking her for allowing me to relive my trips and share my experiences. Now I would like her to have the chance to see firsthand some of the places we've discussed. I can think of no one who would appreciate or benefit more from this opportunity. Bon voyage, Brooke.

She smiled now from her seat at the sidewalk cafe, recalling her shock, as she took a last sip of her lemonade. What an unexpected surprise the legacy had been. Happily, she had been able to convince Mary to accompany her. There had been enough money to cover expenses for two, and they'd had a wonderful time. Brooke knew that as long as she lived she would never forget the decaying elegance of Venice, the awesome majesty of the snow-tipped Swiss Alps, the windmill-dotted landscape of the Netherlands, the incredibly rich and delicious pastries of Germany—the list of memories went on and on.

They'd traveled together until Mary, calling home from Florence to wish her parents a happy anniversary, learned her father had been hospitalized. It hadn't sounded serious, but Mary felt she should be at home with her mother, and Brooke had understood.

She missed Mary's companionship, but she was also enjoying the experience of traveling on her own. And for the next few days, at least, she was looking forward to lying on the beach and soaking up lots of sun.

With a contented sigh, she focused her attention on the sweeping view of the curving coastline and the yacht-dotted sea. Quite a few sailboats were visible from where she sat, and a number of people were wind surfing close to shore. The beach here was rocky, which surprised Brooke, for she had expected the Riviera beaches to consist of vast stretches of gleaming white sand. But if the sunbathers noticed that they were treading on rocks rather than sand, they gave no indication of it.

Anxious for a closer look at the sea, which glittered as if it had been sprinkled with diamonds, she paid her check, hoisted her backpack into place, and set off toward the boardwalk with its well-manicured lawns, colorful flowering bushes, and palm trees. She knew she should delay her walk by the edge of the sea until she'd found a place to stay, but the beckoning crash of the surf was too strong to resist. After all, it didn't hurt to indulge one's whims once in a while, she told herself.

As she ambled along, her gaze swung back and forth

between the sea on her right and the elegant hotels on her left. They were separated from the sea by a wide, impeccably maintained, flower-rimmed boulevard.

The landscape was hilly, and elegant, pastel-colored homes with red tile roofs and decorative wrought iron balconies clung tenaciously to the sides of the hills. The streets wound up the hills like ribbons in a charming, if haphazard, fashion. Brooke smiled from the sheer joy of being a part of this picturesque scene.

Brooke didn't know how long she had been walking, but she was suddenly aware that the shadows of the palm trees had lengthened considerably and that her stomach was quite empty. With a last lingering look, she turned her back on the dazzling, azure expanse and, hoisting her backpack into a more comfortable position, headed into town. She would have to find someone who spoke English or could understand her shaky French and ask them for the name of a nearby tourist-class hotel. Across the street, two women were engaged in conversation, so she decided to try them first.

She had barely started to cross the boulevard when a car on the other side backfired. The loud noise startled Brooke and she jumped, which caused her backpack to slip. As she paused to shift it back into place she also bent down to retrieve her jacket, which had fallen to the street.

Her vision of the street to her left was momentarily obscured at that point, so she was unaware of the car that suddenly appeared from around a curve. By the time she stood up and realized what was happening, the car was upon her. Not until that moment did the driver see her in the dusky light of early evening. Brooke was aware only of the shrill screech of hastily applied brakes and a weird sensation of floating through the air before a dense blackness engulfed her.

16

# *Chapter Two*

The next thing Brooke was aware of was the sound of voices that seemed far away. They blended together into a dull buzz that seemed to be coming from above her. She frowned in puzzlement, keeping her eyes closed as she tried to clear her fuzzy thoughts. Why were the sounds above her? What was going on? Where was she? She opened her eyes, but all she could see were patches of color that moved about, and the harder she tried to focus, the less success she had.

One voice began to rise above the others. As she concentrated on making her thoughts coherent, she heard the voice giving rapid, terse and authoritative commands in French. Slowly, as if from a great distance and through a slightly out-of-focus telescope, she connected the voice to a tall, dark man directly above her. She detected an air of confidence that was clearly communicated by the tone of his voice and his gestures as he spoke to someone in the rapidly gathering crowd.

She frowned, her thoughts still jumbled. She began to realize she was lying in the street, and, flushing uncomfortably at the curious stares of the crowd above her, she struggled to sit up. Immediately the dark-haired man's eyes were on her face and a frown of concern—or was it annoyance?—creased his forehead. He knelt beside her and gently but firmly pushed her back to the pavement.

"Please...I'm all right," she protested, resisting the pressure on her shoulders. She shifted her weight and a sharp pain shot through her leg, a pain so sudden and intense that her eyes widened. A soft, surprised "oh" escaped her lips and her face went a shade paler. She realized that her whole body was trembling.

"I think it would be best if you stayed where you are. An ambulance has been sent for," said the dark-eyed man in perfect English. His voice was smooth and persuasive, with an air of confidence that made Brooke think he must be used to having his orders obeyed. Under normal conditions she probably would have resented his high-handedness, but now his quiet, comforting competence made Brooke feel safe. Wordlessly she gave up the struggle to sit up. She was rewarded for her obedience by a brief, warm smile that foolishly made her tingle all over.

"That's better," said the man, taking her small hand in his own and giving it a gentle squeeze. "The ambulance will be here any minute, and then you'll be away from all these curious stares."

She nodded and smiled tremulously. The knowledge that she had been injured in some way took second place to her amazement at the stranger's sensitivity. It was almost as if he'd read her mind and knew how uncomfortable she felt being the center of attention.

She also gave silent thanks that there was someone in the crowd who spoke English. She cast another surreptitious glance at him, trying to determine his nationality. He looked French in many ways, but he spoke flawless English and actually sounded very much like an American.

A quickly approaching siren caught her attention, and she closed her eyes in relief. Her leg was throbbing now, and the faces of the people in the crowd

18

above her were assuming monstrous proportions. It was almost as if she were looking at them through a fisheye lens.

The crowd parted and two ambulance attendants came through with a stretcher. The dark-eyed man rose and spoke to them in rapid French that Brooke was unable to follow. Then he once more knelt beside her and took her hand in a strong, comforting clasp.

"These men will take you to the hospital now. You're an American, aren't you?"

She nodded. It was frightening to be helpless and alone in a foreign country.

"Don't worry. You'll have the best of care. There's a fine hospital here, and most of the people on staff speak English."

The two attendants moved forward, and though they lifted her gently she had to bite her lip to keep from crying out at the pain that shot through her leg. The dark-eyed man continued to hold her hand until they reached the door of the ambulance, and then he relinquished it.

As the stretcher was placed into the ambulance she strained to get one more glimpse of him. He was at the front of the crowd, one hand casually in the pocket of his elegantly tailored suit, a tall, powerful figure who would stand out in any crowd.

Then the doors were shut, and Brooke experienced a strange emptiness as she lost sight of him. She couldn't explain the reason for that sensation; all she knew was that she wished he was still holding her hand and that his strong, solid presence was beside her.

For the next twenty-four hours, Brooke was either in too much pain or too drugged with pain-killers to be really aware of her surroundings. She was vaguely conscious of pale blue walls, crisp white sheets, and white-coated figures who came and went. Once she even imagined she saw the dark-eyed man standing beside her bed.

When she finally regained full consciousness, however, she found she felt surprisingly well. In fact, except for the heavy elastic bandage that went from mid-calf to mid-thigh, she felt almost as good as new. She said a silent prayer of thanks that the accident had not been any worse.

Now she glanced around the room with interest, noting it had amenities not usually found in hospitals. For one thing, it was a private suite, and the furniture—except for the standard hospital bed—appeared to be made of fine wood. Heavy drapes hung at the large window, beside which stood an easy chair and a reading lamp.

Suddenly Brooke's eye was caught by an overflowing basket of yellow roses that stood on the small table next to the bed. Curiously she reached for the attached card and flipped it open. Written in a scrawling but quite legible hand were the words, "Hope you're feeling better." It was signed "Alan d'Aprix."

The name was unfamiliar to her, and she was frowning with puzzlement when a young nurse with short, curly, black hair popped her head in the door and smiled broadly.

"Well, I am glad to see that you have joined the land of the living again!" she said in accented English. "How are you feeling?"

"Much better," Brooke assured her. "But I'm afraid the details of the past day or so are pretty fuzzy."

"That is to be expected," the nurse said as she straightened a sheet. "You had a very nasty accident. Your knee is wrenched badly and you had a small concussion, but at least nothing is broken. Oh, I see you have noticed the flowers. They are lovely, yes?" she remarked, noting the card in Brooke's hand.

"Yes, they are," Brooke agreed. "But I'm afraid I

20

don't know an Alan d'Aprix. Perhaps they were delivered to the wrong room."

"Oh, no, they are in the right room. They are from the man whose car hit you," the young woman explained. "But of course you do not know him. I am sure there was not time for introductions the night of the accident." Her eyes twinkled with merriment and Brooke smiled in return. "Now, shall I open the blinds for you?" the nurse asked.

"Yes, please."

Sunlight spilled into the room, highlighting the soft sheen of the wood furniture in its path. With a sudden surge of panic, Brooke realized that she must have one of the most expensive rooms in the hospital. How would she ever pay for it? Her trip funds were almost depleted, and she hated to think about dipping into her savings for her return to the United States.

"By the way, my name is Yvonne. If you need anything—Is something wrong?" the nurse asked as she turned from the window and saw Brooke's expression of alarm.

"I suddenly realized that this must be one of your nicest rooms," Brooke said, her voice tense.

"Indeed it is. Monsieur d'Aprix insisted on the best."

"M. d'Aprix?"

"Of course. He is taking care of all your expenses. No need to worry about that."

With a sigh of relief, Brooke sank back on the pillow and closed her eyes. "Thank goodness! I'm afraid this would be out of my price range."

"Well, it is definitely not out of Monsieur d'Aprix's," Yvonne confided. "If you had to be hit by someone, you could not have chosen more wisely. Half the women in Nice—maybe in all of Europe—would gladly throw themselves in front of his car if they thought it would make him notice them. Unfortunately, he seems immune to the charms of the opposite sex—at least on a permanent basis. He always seems to have a different woman on his arm."

"Who is Alan d'Aprix?" Brooke asked curiously. "Do you know him?"

"Ah, mais oui! He's just about the wealthiest and most eligible bachelor in this part of the world." Yvonne rolled her eyes. "He owns several hotels in France, and he has a beautiful home here, plus an apartment in Paris."

"I'd like to thank him for the lovely flowers," said Brooke, fingering the soft petals gently. "Do you have his address or phone number?"

"No one knows his phone number—except perhaps your doctor," Yvonne said. "Everyone knows where he lives, though. But you do not need to worry. He may stop by sometime today. He did last night, a few hours after you were brought in. Then you can thank him in person."

"He's been here?" Brooke asked in surprise. She was touched to think that someone of Alan d'Aprix's apparent importance and power cared enough about her condition to visit the hospital.

"Yes, and his visit was quite an occasion, I can tell you. Word spread quickly that he was here, and every nurse who had a chance came to this floor hoping to get a glimpse of him. His reputation as a ladies' man is quite well known. But I do not think he is *that* wonderful," she remarked. "Besides," she added in a confidential tone, flashing her left hand, which boasted a diamond ring, "I have my own Prince Charming. That is the right term, yes?"

"Yes," Brooke laughed. "You're probably better off, anyway. The playboy type can be pretty unpredictable, I understand. I'm hoping for someone more serious and settled myself." *Someone like the tall, dark-eyed man at the scene of the accident who exuded such quiet competence*, she added silently—then tried determinedly to put him out of her mind. It was idiculous that her heart would beat faster just think-ng about some bystander who stepped forward be-cause he could speak English.

"You haven't seen Monsieur d'Aprix yet," Yvonne warned, her eyes twinkling mischievously.

Brooke shrugged indifferently. "I'm grateful to him for his kindness, of course. But I'm just not attracted to that type." It was true. Brooke preferred men with depth, men who had the capacity to care deeply about one woman and didn't find it necessary to be con-stantly moving from one to another. Only then, she thought, would she have that spiritual union Mrs. Bates had talked about and her parents had shared.

"Well, perhaps it will be good for him to find a woman who is immune to his charms," Yvonne said thoughtfully, studying Brooke. Then she laughed. "At least it will be a novel experience for him!" She reached over and straightened the last crease in the sheet. "Now, is there anything I can get for you? The doctor will be in soon."

"I am a little hungry," said Brooke, suddenly aware of the hollow feeling in her stomach.

"I am not surprised. It has been a long time since you have eaten. I will see about getting you something right away."

"Oh, Yvonne—" Brooke stopped her as she started to leave. "I must look awful." She ran her hand dis-tractedly through her hair. "Do you suppose you could find me a brush or comb and a mirror? I had some things in my backpack."

"Ah, you must be feeling better. Très bien!" Yvonne smiled. "But I am afraid there was not much left of your backpack," she informed Brooke. "Monsieur d'A-prix took what there was to keep for you until you were well enough to need your things. But I will see what I can do."

"Thank you. I'd hate to have anyone see me like this."

"Well, after all, it is only Monsieur d'Aprix," said Yvonne innocently. "And you said you did not care about him."

"I'm not doing this for him," Brooke said, blushing. "I'll just feel better when my hair is combed."

"Oh, but of course. I should have known." Yvonne winked at her and closed the door.

It was true, of course, that Brooke didn't care what Alan d'Aprix thought of her. Still, she'd never met anyone from that stratum of society. *It's only natural to want to look one's best when meeting someone new,* she told herself defensively.

Having been warned of M. d'Aprix's so-called "irresistible" charms by Yvonne, Brooke was determined not to be overly impressed by him. He was probably conceited and overbearing anyway, so it shouldn't be too hard to carry through with her plan. She had never been impressed with people who were impressed with themselves.

Brooke's musings were interrupted by the appearance of an orderly bearing a tray of food, and she greeted him with a smile, taking an appreciative whiff at the same time.

"Bon appétit!" he said as he turned to leave.

"Merci," she called after him, and then surveyed the appetizing tray hungrily. Although she'd never been in a hospital before, she'd heard horror stories about hospital fare. But this was obviously several notches above typical hospital food. A fluffy omelet stuffed with ham was flanked by two generous wedges of melon. A large, flaky croissant was on a separate plate, and golden butter and strawberry jam were in small crocks. A pot of steaming coffee and a glass of orange juice were also included.

Brooke sighed in ecstasy as she quickly buttered the croissant and took a big bite of the tender omelet. While she ate, she glanced around the attractive room again. *If this is the kind of treatment wealthy people*

24

*receive, it might not be so bad to have money*, she thought with gleeful impudence.

Brooke was just finishing the last delicious morsel when Yvonne returned, triumphantly brandishing a brush, comb, and mirror.

"Look what I found," she said.

"Oh, Yvonne, thank you! Where did you get them?"

"There is a little gift shop here in the hospital. They have all sorts of things there," she replied as she moved the stand away from the bed and surveyed the empty plate. "You were not too hungry, were you?" she teased.

"No, not at all." Brooke grinned wryly. "Just starving. How much do I owe you for these things?" she asked as Yvonne laid her purchases on the bed.

"Nothing at all. Monsieur d'Aprix said you were to have everything you needed and we are just to add the cost to your bill."

"Oh, but I can't let him pay for things like this."

"Why not?" Yvonne asked pragmatically. "His car ran over your backpack and destroyed your things. The least he can do is replace them. Besides, for a woman these things are a necessity."

"Still, I hate to be in his debt...." Brooke frowned.

"Ma chérie!" Yvonne rolled her eyes and threw up her hands dramatically. "A man practically kills you with his car and you are worried about his paying for a few little items? It is the least he can do!"

Brooke smiled in amusement at the other woman's theatrical tone and gestures. She supposed Yvonne was right. "Okay. No more protests. Do you think you could help me sit up a little now?"

"Of course." Yvonne adjusted the bed, and Brooke felt a twinge of pain as her leg moved. The nurse glanced up when she noticed the involuntary tightening of her patient's muscles. "Does your knee hurt?"

"A little," admitted Brooke.

"That is only normal, of course. But the pain will

25

get less and less. If it really begins to trouble you, though, let me know. There." Yvonne returned from the end of the bed and placed the brush, comb, and mirror within Brooke's reach. "If you need anything else, just press that button." She indicated a small disc next to the bed.

"Thank you. I will," Brooke promised.

When Yvonne had gone, Brooke elevated the mirror and stared at her reflection. Her face looked a bit thinner and much paler than it had two days ago, and her hair was a tangled mass. She made a face at herself and began to work furiously with the brush until at last the strands of her hair had regained their usual soft silkiness and fell in graceful waves around her face.

There wasn't much she could do about her pale appearance, though. She normally used few cosmetics, but a bit of blush and some lipstick would certainly improve her looks. She should have asked Yvonne to purchase some for her. Oh, well, too late now.

As she was placing the brush and mirror on the table next to the bed, the door opened and a portly, mustached man in white with a jolly face and a stethoscope around his neck entered.

"Bonjour, mademoiselle. I am Dr. Lafitte. Your nurse tells me that you are feeling much better today." He smiled pleasantly, and Brooke took an immediate liking to him.

"Yes, thank you. Am I all right, doctor?"

"Soon you will be as good as new," he assured her. Though his accent was much heavier than Yvonne's, Brooke had no trouble understanding him. "You know, of course, about the wrenched knee. It is rather nasty, but we will have you on crutches this afternoon. You also have a slight concussion, but," he made a gesture of dismissal with his hand, "it is nothing to be concerned about. I would suggest rest for a few days, and then you can resume your normal activities. But

26

no jogging," he said in mock seriousness, shaking his finger at her. She laughed.

"I don't even do that when I'm well," she assured him.

"Ah, then there is nothing to worry about." He gave the empty breakfast tray a quick glance. "I see your appetite is fine. That is a good sign. If everything goes well today, you may leave tomorrow. You will be in this area for a few days?"

"Well, I'd really like to go back to England since I won't be able to do any sightseeing. Is that a problem?"

"It would be best to rest for a few days before embarking on any strenuous travel," the doctor explained. "Your body has had quite a shock. I would like to take another look at that knee in a few days, and you should give your body a little time to regain its strength. Would it be possible to remain a short time?"

"Yes, I guess so." There really was no hurry to get back to England. Besides, she did feel a bit weak.

"Good. I think that will be best. Now, we will have a look."

He gave her a thorough exam, and when he finished he helped her readjust the hospital gown. "You are looking very well," he told her. "In a few days, after I see you again, you will be ready to travel. Your own doctor in England can take care of you then. Oh, Monsieur d'Aprix has taken care of notifying your relatives about the accident, I believe. He said he would do that the night you were brought in, and he is a very thorough man. So I am sure they have been told, in case you are worried."

"There's really no one to tell," Brooke said. "I lost my parents three years ago, and my roommate is away from London right now. I hope he didn't go to too much trouble trying to locate someone. I'm afraid I've caused quite a bother as it is."

"Do not worry, mademoiselle. It was not your

fault," the doctor patted her hand.

"It may have been," Brooke replied, her face troubled. "I don't remember the accident very clearly, but I might have stepped out in front of him." She frowned, trying to recall the sequence of events. A knock on the door broke her reverie, however.

"Come in," the doctor called.

Brooke could only stare incredulously at the figure who stepped through the door. Her memory of the accident might have been fuzzy, but one thing stood out clearly—the dark-eyed man who had held her hand while she lay on the pavement and who had spoken to her in such understanding tones. Though he was dressed in a different—but equally elegant—suit, she had no doubt that the man now standing in the doorway was the same man to whose hand she had gratefully clung while awaiting the ambulance. As if through a fog, she heard the doctor speak.

"Well, if you are concerned about whether you caused the accident, here is the man to ask, Mademoiselle Peyton. This is Alan d'Aprix."

## Chapter Three

Brooke could hardly believe her eyes. The kind stranger from the scene of the accident was Alan d'Aprix! And she had thought him simply to be a passer-by who had come to her assistance!

Suddenly she became aware that she was staring openly at him, and she saw that he was looking at her with an expression of tolerant amusement. Hot color flushed her cheeks, and she lowered her eyes. He walked toward her with an easy grace, and he extended his hand.

"I'm pleased to meet you, Miss Peyton, although I wish it had been under more pleasant circumstances." His voice was deep and resonant, and Brooke looked up once more into those—gray, she noted—eyes and placed her hand in his. He took it in a firm clasp, and she was reminded once more of how comforted she had felt when he'd taken her hand at the scene of the accident. Now he held it just a moment longer than necessary, and Brooke's heart began to beat faster as his intense eyes smiled into hers. She berated herself for being a fool, but she had to admit that she liked the way he made her feel. Too bad she couldn't have been dressed in something more flattering than a stark white, shapeless hospital gown, or had some makeup on to help camouflage the paleness of her face.

At last he released her hand, and Brooke finally found her voice.

"It's nice to meet you, too, M. d'Aprix." She was amazed at how calm and controlled she sounded. "But as Dr. Lafitte said, I'm not too clear about how the accident happened. So I don't know whether to be angry or to apologize."

"Neither, I hope," he replied smoothly. "Let's just say it was a combination of circumstances. It was dusk, so visibility was low. You were bent down in the middle of the street, and I was driving a bit too fast." He shrugged. "In any case, let's just be thankful that the results weren't more serious—although I realize that a badly wrenched knee is not exactly minor." He smiled, and the firm, aggressive lines of his mouth softened. Brooke could not help but respond to the warmth in his eyes, and she returned the smile.

"Well, as you said, it could have been worse. In fact, Dr. Lafitte said I could leave tomorrow." Determinedly she tried to slow the rapid beating of her heart. What was the matter with her?

Alan d'Aprix turned to the doctor, and for the first time since he'd entered the room Brooke was able to study him unobserved. His light charcoal-gray suit complimented his eyes, and he wore it with the natural air of style possessed by only a fortunate few. The suit was obviously expensive and custom-tailored, for it perfectly accentuated his taut, muscular frame.

Her scrutiny continued to his face, now in profile, and she noted the strong jawline, the aquiline nose, and the carefully styled hair. He looked to be in his early thirties. Yvonne had been right. He exuded a magnetism that was almost tangible. No wonder women were attracted to him! She sensed that he could be a formidable opponent in certain situations, though he had been most considerate and kind to her. She suspected that no one got the better of Alan d'A-prix in a business deal, and that once he made up his

30

mind to have something, very little stood in his way.

"Is that right, doctor? Will you be releasing Miss Peyton tomorrow?" His voice interrupted her thoughts.

"I see no reason to hold her any longer. She is basically a very healthy young woman." He glanced her way and smiled. "Now, I have to complete my rounds, so if you will excuse me…"

"Of course. And thank you, doctor." Alan d'Aprix shook his hand, and the doctor bowed slightly.

"My pleasure."

He watched the doctor leave, and then turned once more to Brooke.

"How do you feel today? I must say you look a great deal better than you did yesterday when I stopped by." As he spoke he sat down in the chair next to the window and casually crossed one leg over the other.

"I feel very well, actually," Brooke replied, conscious of his penetrating eyes on her face. "I must thank you, M. d'Aprix—"

"Alan," he corrected her.

"Alan," she conceded, "for arranging for this lovely room. It wasn't at all necessary. And one of the nurses told me that you are taking care of all the bills. I'm grateful."

He waved her thanks aside. "It was the least I could do after so rudely interrupting your vacation. I take it this was a holiday?"

She nodded. "I was almost ready to go back, though. I was just going to spend a few days here and a few in Paris and then go back to London."

"By the way, I did try to call the London number I found among your belongings, but I got no answer. And I tried—unsuccessfully—to track down a phone number in the States for the address on your passport. I finally cabled, but there's been no answer yet."

"There won't be," Brooke informed him. "My roommate in London is away, so the apartment there is empty. And the address in the States is...was my parents' home. They were killed in a car accident three years ago," she explained softly, lowering her eyes.

"I'm sorry," said Alan simply, but with compassion in his voice, and Brooke thanked him for his understanding with a tremulous smile.

"I suppose I should be able to handle it better by now, but I loved them very much."

Alan gave her a thoughtful look. "Don't apologize for caring deeply. Too few people do."

Brooke looked at him curiously. That remark had been made sincerely and had obviously been meant as a compliment. It did not fit the mental image she had drawn of this wealthy, attractive jet-setter. But before she had time to consider it further, he continued.

"Then I take it there is no one who needs to be notified?"

"No."

"What about a traveling companion?"

"I was traveling with a friend, but she had to leave suddenly. So I was going to continue the trip alone."

A frown crossed his forehead, and he stood up. At first Brooke thought he was preparing to leave, and her heart sank. There was something about just being in his presence that made her feel safe and protected. But he simply walked to the window and stood gazing out. He seemed to be debating something in his mind. At last he turned and addressed her. "What are you planning to do tomorrow when you're released?"

The question took Brooke off guard, and she looked at him in confusion for a moment. "Well, I guess I'll get a room. The doctor asked me to stay in town for a few days so he could check my knee again before I left. He said that as long as I wasn't pressed to get back to London he would prefer that I stay here and rest. I'd planned to spend some time here, anyway, so I don't mind. I just won't be able to do much sightseeing."

"How will you manage alone?" he asked.

"I'm sure once I get the hang of the crutches I'll be fine," she assured him with faint surprise. She hadn't expected his solicitude to extend this far.

"You'll need some help to get around, at least for a few days." He paused and then said matter-of-factly, "You may recuperate at my home."

Brooke stared at him in disbelief. If Yvonne had told her the truth—and she had no reason to doubt the nurse—this man was considered to be the playboy of the Riviera. And now he was inviting her to be a guest in his house! Of course, she had no illusions that he had any interest in her as a woman. He was just being kind to her from a sense of duty. Actually, he probably considered the whole affair to be a nuisance. Still...

"What's the matter?" he asked, and she realized that she'd been staring again.

"Well, I appreciate the invitation, but it's just that...I really can manage...and I don't know if it would be proper....I've heard you're...not married," she finished lamely, her face crimson.

"Proper!" His eyes filled with laughter, and Brooke turned even redder. "My goodness, you are an old-fashioned girl!"

"I guess I am," she replied stiffly, looking at him proudly. She wasn't ashamed of her values, but she knew they were incomprehensible to some of her contemporaries. "Besides, I wasn't just thinking of myself," she added defensively.

"Brooke, if you're insinuating that you don't want to hurt my reputation, I can assure you that you needn't worry. My reputation is well established—truthfully or not." His eyes clouded darkly for a moment before he continued. "So one more young woman won't make any difference."

*I'll bet it won't*, she thought, hurt and angry at the same time.

"But if it will make you feel any better," he continued, "we will have a chaperon. Two, in fact. I have a

33

housekeeper and a gardener. So we won't be alone in the house."

She looked up and saw the glint of amusement in his eyes and bit her lip. He must think her a naive fool. Suddenly she wondered if he had interpreted her remark as flirtatious. She looked at him in alarm, and again he read her eyes.

"Now what is that busy brain of yours thinking?" he teased.

She lowered her eyes, her long lashes sweeping her cheeks. How could she tell him she hadn't intended her remarks to be a come-on? For some reason it was vital to her that he know her concerns had been sincere.

"I hope you didn't think I was trying to...suggest anything," she said carefully. Silence greeted her comment, a silence that stretched uncomfortably. Finally, unable to wait any longer for his reaction, she looked up to find Alan staring at her pensively.

Brooke's fingers played with the sheet as she endured his scrutiny, but her eyes met his directly, never wavering. When at last he spoke, his voice was serious, and his eyes had lost their teasing light.

"I'm sure the concerns you expressed were just that—concerns, not an invitation. My reputation has obviously preceded me, but you may believe me when I tell you that I'm not quite the lecher you've apparently been led to expect. You have my solemn word that while you are a guest in my house you will be perfectly safe—in every way. With that understanding, will you agree to come for a few days, until you recover enough to travel?"

Brooke met his eyes, saw the sincerity in them, and knew, intuitively, that she could trust this man not to break his word. Mutely she nodded. He smiled and gave her hand a gentle squeeze.

"Good. I'll come by and pick you up tomorrow. Meanwhile, I'll have some clothes sent to you. I'm afraid your things aren't in very good shape." He released her hand and walked toward the door, pausing when he reached it to look back, an enigmatic smile on his face. "I'll see you tomorrow."

Brooke spent the afternoon learning how to use her crutches, a skill she soon decided would require a great deal of practice to perfect. She was rapidly coming to the conclusion that she'd made the correct decision in accepting Alan d'Aprix's offer of a place to stay for a few days. Not only was she having trouble maneuvering with the crutches, but she was also surprisingly weak. She had been working only a few minutes with the cumbersome supports before she had to let Yvonne help her back into bed.

"I can't understand what's the matter with me," she complained. "I feel so weak, and my muscles are like jelly."

"You will soon be back to normal," Yvonne assured her. "Your body has had quite a shock and it needs time to adjust. Just plan to take it easy for the next few days. That should not be a problem. I am sure that anyone who stays with Alan d'Aprix is waited on— what is the expression?…ah, oui, I remember—hand and foot."

Brooke settled herself more comfortably in the bed and leaned over to adjust the covers, embarrassingly aware the Yvonne wasn't the only one who knew about Alan's invitation. She didn't know how the word had spread, but apparently everyone in the hospital had heard that she would be spending the next few days at Alan d'Aprix's home. Well, what did she care? she asked herself defiantly. Alan d'Aprix was simply being kind, out of a sense of responsibility, to someone he had injured. That was all there was to it.

"Do not worry, you will get the hang of the crutches," Yvonne said. "By tomorrow you will be an expert."

That wasn't quite true, but at least Brooke felt a bit more confident after several more practice sessions. In fact, when Yvonne came in early the next morning carrying a stack of boxes of various sizes, Brooke was handling the crutches quite well as she practiced walking around the room.

"Very good." Yvonne nodded approvingly as she deposited the boxes on the bed and placed her hands on her hips. "Soon you will have them mastered."

"I doubt that," said Brooke as she carefully lowered herself into the easy chair by the window. "But at least I'll be able to get around by myself. What are those?" she asked curiously, indicating the boxes.

"They are for you. And from the name on the boxes, I would say they are clothes—and very nice clothes, too. Were you expecting something?" she asked with interest.

"M. d'Aprix said he'd send some things over," Brooke replied casually as she pushed herself to her feet. "My clothes were all ruined, you know, and I don't think I can leave the hospital in this." She glanced down at the voluminous hospital gown with a grimace as she made her way toward the bed. "I hope they fit. M. d'Aprix didn't even ask my size."

"He probably checked the labels in your old clothes," Yvonne pointed out. "But I doubt whether he even needed to do that. I am sure he could tell by looking at you what size you wear." Yvonne either didn't see or chose to ignore Brooke's startled expression, for she continued immediately. "Would you like some help getting dressed?"

"I think I can manage. But thank you."

After Yvonne left, Brooke sat down on the bed and eagerly began to open the boxes. She was going to enjoy these clothes to the fullest. After all, Alan d'Aprix had destroyed her own clothes, and there was nothing wrong with accepting these replacements. Certainly they were of much better quality than her jeans and simple tops, but...

Brooke gasped as she removed the last layer of tissue paper, revealing the garment inside. Tenderly she lifted the linen dress from the box. It was a delicate shade of green, sleeveless, with a square neckline that was adorned with graceful, intricate embroidery. It was cinched tightly at the waist by a belt and the full skirt flared out in a wide arc.

Brooke had never had anything quite like it in her life. Her father's salary as a history professor at a small midwestern college had not allowed for the luxury of truly elegant clothes. His legacy to her had not been material goods, but constant love, deep-seated faith, and joy in the study of history. Those gifts were still the ones she treasured, but she couldn't help but delight in the beautiful dress.

Carefully Brooke laid it on the bed and turned her attention to the other boxes. White sandals and a matching purse were in two of them, and a small but complete makeup kit was in another.

One small box remained, and Brooke placed it on her lap curiously, noting as she opened it that it was very light. She pushed aside the tissue and then felt hot color rise in her cheeks when she realized that the box contained pale beige, silk lingerie. She wondered fleetingly if Alan d'Aprix had chosen it.

*Don't be silly*, she admonished herself. *He's much too busy to concern himself with something like this*. Remembering Yvonne's comment about his perceptive eye for sizes, she glanced at the tags and noted that all the sizes were correct. Could he really tell just by looking? *Of course not*, she chided herself. He probably just had someone check the sizes on her old things. And what did it matter, anyway? All she wanted to do was try on these lovely things.

Just as she reached behind her neck to untie the

37

sack-like hospital gown, Dr. Lafitte came in, followed by Yvonne.

"My goodness, it looks like a birthday!" he exclaimed with a smile.

"It feels like one," Brooke agreed. "Aren't they lovely?"

"Indeed they are. And as soon as I finish my exam you may put them on. Shall we proceed?"

A few minutes later he nodded with satisfaction as he made some notes on her chart. "You are looking very well. A few days' rest and you will be almost back to normal. The knee will take a little longer to heal, of course, but even that will be better soon. You may leave whenever you are ready, and I will see you next week, yes?"

"Yes. I'll be staying with M. d'Aprix for a few days."

"Good. You will be close by if you should need me." He gave a small bow and left, followed by Yvonne, who paused at the door to wink.

"Enjoy your new things. They are lovely."

Brooke smiled in reply, and the moment the door was closed, she gathered up the clothes and headed for the bathroom, anxious to see if everything fit.

Emerging a few minutes later, she paused to glance at herself in the mirror. The clothes did fit—as if they had been designed for her, in fact—and the tightly cinched waist of the dress emphasized her own small waist.

She had brushed her hair until it shone, and it now fell in soft waves around her face and onto her shoulders. She felt much better with lipstick and blush on, although the blush was hardly necessary over the faint flush of excitement in her cheeks.

She was still standing there when a knock sounded on the door, and, startled, Brooke called, "Come in."

Alan d'Aprix entered and glanced toward the bed. When he saw that it was empty his puzzled eyes swept the room, coming to rest almost immediately on the slender woman in pale green who was balanced on crutches, her eyes wide and her generous lips slightly parted in surprise.

Brooke thought she heard a sharply indrawn breath. She stood still, not daring to move as Alan's eyes took in every detail of her appearance. He seemed in some way to be deeply affected by what he saw, and for some reason she was almost afraid to breathe. At last she forced herself to speak.

"Do I pass?" she asked lightly, forcing herself to smile.

Her question broke the awkward silence, and Alan, realizing that he had been staring, made a visible effort to compose his face. When he spoke, his tone was as light as hers. "I'm surprised to see you up," he remarked, ignoring her question. "Are you feeling better today?"

"Much," she nodded, moving toward the bed. Under his gaze, she felt awkward on the crutches, and she was sure she looked quite clumsy. "They tell me I'll get used to these, but I'm not so sure," she commented wryly as she carefully sat on the edge of the bed, leaning the crutches against the mattress next to her.

"I see the clothes fit." His eyes again swept her quickly but thoroughly. "You look very nice—quite a bit different from the last time I saw you. That green does much more for your complexion than the white hospital gown did."

"Thank you," she murmured, not quite sure how to respond. "I really appreciate all the trouble you've gone to. But I don't feel quite right about accepting such beautiful clothes. I know they must have been terribly expensive."

"Don't worry about it," he waved her protest aside. "Just enjoy them. I certainly am."

Brooke glanced down. Why did he make her feel so much like a schoolgirl? And why did her heart hammer so heavily in her chest every time he looked at her? Why did her breathing suddenly become shallow and quick? Surely she was too old to be subject to the symptoms of a teen-age crush. Suddenly she realized that he was still standing, and she flushed hotly.

"I'm so sorry. Won't you sit down?"

"Actually, if you're ready, I thought we'd leave. Hospitals aren't my favorite places, and it's much too nice a day to waste inside."

"Of course," she said, nodding. *I'm probably keeping him from some important appointment as it is. Since I'm already imposing on his hospitality, I shouldn't take up his time, too,* she added silently. Putting the crutches once more under her arms, she stood up. "I'm ready. Do I need to sign out or anything?"

"No. I've already talked with Dr. Lafitte and he's signed your release. Just a moment, and I'll see if I can find a nurse so we can get a wheelchair for you."

"Oh, I really don't—" But he had already disappeared through the door. She shrugged. She suspected it was useless to argue with Alan d'Aprix once he made up his mind. Besides, she couldn't use the crutches well enough yet to navigate any long distances. The wheelchair was probably a good idea.

She didn't have long to wait. Alan was back almost immediately, followed by Yvonne, who helped Brooke into the chair. Alan took the crutches.

"I feel like such an invalid," Brooke said in embarrassment.

"Well, you have a legitimate reason to be pampered for awhile," Yvonne declared, and she leaned closer so only Brooke could hear. "And you may as well enjoy it!"

Brooke gave her a warm open smile. It might be a great adventure at that.

## Chapter Four

Brooke could not help but feel uncomfortable, though, as the three of them made their way down the hospital corridor under the curious gazes of the hospital staff. When at last they emerged into the sunlight, she breathed a sigh of relief and glanced covertly at Alan, but he seemed oblivious to the stares and whispers. Well, she supposed he was used to being in the spotlight. For her it was a new—and distasteful—experience.

"Here we are," said Yvonne gaily, interrupting her thoughts. They'd stopped at the curb next to an obviously expensive, low-slung sports car which was a rich cream color with chocolate-colored upholstery. In fact, it had probably cost more than whatever her annual salary would be when she got a job back in the States. Alan d'Aprix must be very wealthy indeed.

Yvonne helped her to her feet, and Alan, who had deposited her crutches in the trunk, joined them on the passenger side of the car. He smiled at Yvonne.

"Thank you for your help. I think we can manage now."

"Très bien, monsieur."

"Thank you, Yvonne. You've been a great help," Brooke added warmly.

"It was my pleasure." Yvonne smiled and waved as

41

she turned to push the wheelchair back inside.

"Shall we go?" Alan asked pleasantly, turning back to Brooke. She nodded and lowered herself into the car, swinging her left leg in. Then she stared at her right leg. There was no graceful way to get it inside. The strain of swinging it in would hurt too much. Alan obviously realized her dilemma, for he quickly reached down and gently lifted her leg inside. Then he closed the door and made his way around to the driver's side. He slid into place and started the engine before he glanced at her.

"Comfortable?"

"Yes, very. This is the most luxurious car I've ever been in!" It was true. The upholstery was real leather, and the cushions were incredibly soft. The tinted windows not only cut down the glare from outside, but also acted as a privacy shield for the occupants. Brooke sighed with pleasure. She would probably never again be treated to such luxury.

"Is something wrong?" Alan inquired sharply, apparently misinterpreting her sigh.

"Oh, no," she assured him quickly with a smile. "I'm just not used to such beautiful things. First these clothes, and now this car..." She leaned back and closed her eyes. "I'm sure you must think I'm very unsophisticated, but I can't help it. To me these things are a real treat." She opened her eyes and turned her head to smile at him. "I can't tell you how much I appreciate your hospitality."

"I'm glad you're pleased. And you are unsophisticated—in the nicest sense of the word. You seem in many ways to be untouched by the world, unaffected by the crass commercialism that we see so much of now. I find that refreshing." He smiled at her warmly, and she lowered her gaze, a faint smile on her lips. She was flattered by his remarks, sure that Alan d'Aprix did not give compliments lightly.

They drove in silence for a few minutes, and Brooke

was absorbed in watching the scenery. At the moment they were high above the sea on a curving coastal road. Here the cliffs rose sharply from the sea, and the road was perched on a narrow shelf of land about midway up, giving Brooke an unobstructed view of a few sailboats dotted here and there on the sparkling, cerulean expanse.

"It's absolutely gorgeous here!" she exclaimed. "I've always heard that the Riviera was lovely, but I had no idea it was anything like this."

"It is beautiful," he agreed, "but it's become a bit crowded in recent years. That's why I only live here a short time each year."

"Where is your real home?" Brooke asked.

"You mean where do I spend most of my time, or where was I born?"

"Both, I guess," Brooke replied. "You look rather French, but you sound like an American."

"My father was French and my mother is an American," he answered easily. "They separated years ago, and my father stayed in France where he owned several hotels. My mother went back to the States—Boston—and I went with her. So I grew up in America, although I always spent the summers with my father. When he died a few years ago I took over the hotels. Now I spend part of each year here and part in the States. I suppose I consider the United States my real home—and I do have a house there—but I feel just as comfortable in France."

"It must have been hard growing up without both parents there," Brooke mused. Her home had been so loving, so filled with happiness, that her heart went out to those who had never experienced that kind of environment. Brooke's mother had always been there when she got home from school, waiting with freshly baked cookies or cake to hear about Brooke's day, as if algebra tests and spelling bees were the most fascinating subjects in the world. And her father had never

43

been too busy to answer her persistent, eager questions or to fix a broken bicycle.

"It wasn't always easy having my parents on different sides of the Atlantic," Alan admitted. "I loved them both deeply, but for a long time I resented them for not making their marriage work. At least I wasn't subjected to an awful divorce scandal. They ended their marriage gracefully—or as gracefully as possible—in a dignified, quiet manner, and I was always thankful for that. An ugly divorce can damage a child so much."

He paused as he concentrated on negotiating a particularly sharp curve. "I finally accepted the situation. I stayed on good terms with both of my parents, and I still see Mother frequently. But after their breakup I resolved never to enter into marriage hastily. If I marry, I want it to last forever."

Brooke digested his words thoughtfully, surprised at the intensity in his voice. When the silence lengthened he turned to her and raised one eyebrow.

"Any more questions?" he asked pleasantly. She shook her head.

"I hope you didn't think I was prying."

"Of course not. It's only logical to want to know something about one's host. Besides, if it will make you feel any better, you can tell me about yourself later." He turned the car in sharply toward the curb and stopped. Brooke glanced out the window with interest. They were in front of a building with an awning that discreetly bore the name of the shop from which Brooke's clothes had come. She turned to him questioningly.

"Where are we?"

"Madame Barry's," he said, indicating the shop.

"But why are we here?" she asked in puzzlement. "These clothes fit fine."

"That's precisely why we're here," he replied patiently, his sensual mouth curving slighty upward.

"I'm afraid I don't understand."

44

"Well, you certainly don't expect to wear that same dress for the next several days, do you?"

"Oh." He was right, of course. But she was sure that the small amount of money she had left wouldn't go very far in this shop. And she needed what remained of her bequest to get back to England. How could she tactfully suggest a less expensive shop?

"These will, of course, be put on my account," Alan said matter-of-factly. "They are simply a replacement for the rest of your clothes."

"Oh, no, I can't let you do that," she protested.

"Why not?" he asked smoothly.

"Well…it just isn't right," she finished lamely. "I've put you to too much expense already."

"Nonsense," he dismissed her protest curtly. "Don't try to get out until I come around."

Brooke remained where she was, uncomfortably aware that she couldn't very well start an argument with him in the middle of the sidewalk. Apparently he thought he owed her the clothes. And she did need more than one outfit for the week.

Finding no quick solution to the problem, she decided to accept his generosity. But she would be as frugal as possible in her purchases—or as frugal as the shop allowed, she thought wryly, glancing at the unobtrusive but elegant exterior of the exclusive shop.

Alan opened the door on her side, and before she could say a word he had reached into the car, lifted her out, and set her on her feet, leaving her to cling in surprise to the open door while he retrieved her crutches from the trunk. The maneuver had been accomplished so smoothly and quickly that she had hardly been aware of the moment that she was in his arms. But the faint impression of a strong body pressed tightly against her own was almost dizzying. He handed her the crutches, seemingly unaware that only a few seconds before she had been in his arms.

"Can you manage all right?"

"I think so," she said a bit breathlessly, putting the crutches under her arms and trying to calm her thudding heart.

"I don't want to tire you. The doctor said you needed rest for the next couple of days. But I thought a brief stop here was a good idea. Madame Barry could have sent some more things over, but most women seem to like to select their own clothes. You do feel up to it, don't you?" he asked, a concerned frown creasing his brow.

"Oh, yes. Actually, I feel fine."

"Good." His face relaxed and he gently guided her toward the front of the shop, his hand protectively resting on her waist to shield her from any accidental bumps from pedestrians hurrying past. Again his touch caused a strange, disturbing sensation in her spine.

Brooke had been right about the shop. The room they entered was thickly carpeted, with a few antique chairs and couches placed at random. A couple of dresses were discreetly displayed, but no other clothes were in evidence. Even in the shop where Brooke had worked in London the clothes had been on display. She looked around with interest, and a moment later an elegantly dressed older woman appeared from behind a curtain at the rear of the shop.

"Ah, Monsieur d'Aprix. Bonjour."

"Bonjour, Madame Barry. This is Brooke Peyton, about whom I spoke to you."

"Ah, oui. Bonjour, mademoiselle. The clothes—they fit well, yes?" she asked with a smile, surveying Brooke with an expert eye.

"Yes. They're just beautiful," Brooke replied, returning the smile.

"Très bien." The woman nodded in satisfaction.

"I have some business to attend to, Madame Barry. I'll leave Brooke in your hands. She needs a few more things, as we discussed. I'll be back in—" he paused and glanced at his watch—"two hours. Will that give you enough time? I don't want to tire Miss Peyton. She's just out of the hospital."

"That will be fine," the woman assured him. Already she had taken charge and was leading Brooke to a couch. "We will accomplish much in that time."

Two hours had never passed more swiftly. And Brooke had never seen so many lovely clothes. She would have liked to buy dozens of things, but she limited herself to the bare essentials. She wouldn't take advantage of Alan's generosity, despite Madame Barry's urging.

"But mademoiselle, Monsieur d'Aprix will be most upset if you buy so few things," she protested. "He said you were to have everything you needed."

"But this is all I need," Brooke said firmly. "I'll only be here a few days." She had already bought another dress, two pairs of slacks, several tops and skirts, a swimsuit, a nightgown, robe, slippers, a pair of casual shoes, and some lingerie. They would do nicely for the next week, and she didn't plan to impose on Alan's hospitality any longer than that.

"Well, if you insist," the owner said, obviously unconvinced. Brooke smiled to herself. Madame Barry was probably accustomed to selling clothes to people who changed outfits several times a day.

"This will be just fine," Brooke assured her again. "And I appreciate all your help. The clothes are exquisite."

"Merci," the woman smiled. "It was our pleasure to serve you. You have such a perfect figure that you are a joy to dress. May I get you something to drink while you wait for Monsieur d'Aprix?"

"No, I think I'll just rest," Brooke said, leaning back on the couch. She couldn't believe how tired she had grown in just the last few minutes.

True to his word, Alan was back at the shop within five minutes of the time he had promised. She had a moment to study him unobserved before his eyes adjusted to the dim interior of the shop, and she once again found her pulses fluttering as her gaze swept his lean, muscular frame. She traced the strong outlines of his handsome face and was once again aware that the man exuded an almost tangible magnetism. It was no wonder that he could have his choice of women.

At last his eyes came to rest on her, and his face relaxed into an easy smile as he strode toward her. At the same moment Madame Barry appeared from the rear of the shop.

"Oh, Monsieur d'Aprix, we have just finished," she said.

"Good. Did you get everything you needed?" he asked, turning his attention to Brooke.

"Yes," she said, nodding.

"Actually, mademoiselle was most conservative in her purchases," Madame Barry informed him. "I encouraged her to buy more, but..." she threw up her hands.

"Is that true, Brooke?" Alan asked, turning back to her with a frown.

"Well, I'll only be here for a few days," she pointed out, feeling somewhat intimidated by the figure towering over her.

Brooke was unable to read his thoughts, but his eyes regarded her in an almost calculating manner, and she wondered if he were displeased. But why should he be? If anything, she had saved him money. Besides, her knee was beginning to throb. What she really wanted to do was lie down, not argue.

Finally Alan turned to Madame Barry. "I'm sure Miss Peyton has everything she needs at the moment. If she finds later that she's missing something, I'll see that she returns."

Brooke wasn't sure if she liked his imperious, "I'll see that she returns," but she was too tired to object. In any case, considering the way she was feeling right now it was rather nice to have someone else take charge of the situation.

"Ready, Brooke?"

She glanced up and nodded, forcing herself to smile. Alan's eyes scrutinized her face, and without comment he reached down, gently helped her to her feet, and handed her the crutches.

Alan didn't speak again until he had helped Brooke into the car and taken his place behind the wheel. As he pulled into traffic, he turned to her with a look of concern.

"Are you feeling well, Brooke? You look rather pale. Is your knee bothering you?"

"A bit," she confessed, not wanting to admit that both it and her head were throbbing painfully.

"I haven't known you very long, Brooke, but I have a feeling that you've just made a rather large understatement."

"Am I that bad an actress?" she inquired, giving up the pretense of feeling wonderful. She apparently wasn't fooling Alan anyway.

"No. You're just a young woman who's had a rather nasty accident and is tired after a morning of shopping. I think the best thing for you right now is rest."

Brooke nodded in silent agreement. She leaned back in the seat and closed her eyes, not even having enough energy to enjoy the spectacular coastal scenery. She could feel the car climbing, but she didn't open her eyes until the vehicle slowed and made a sharp right turn.

The car seemed at first to be poised on the edge of a precipice far above the sea. She caught her breath sharply before she realized that at the edge of the road a wrought iron gate was swinging open as Alan pushed a button on the dashboard. Could there actually be a house perched on these cliffs?

Moments later Brooke discovered that the dwelling below them, which they approached via a slanted, curving drive, was not a house—it was a villa! At least that was how she would describe it. Constructed of an adobe-like material and painted a pale rose color, the structure nestled into the hill on several levels. Vivid scarlet and purple bougainvillea clung to the walls in graceful patterns, and roses, oleander, and tropical greenery were in abundance, some plants almost as high as the red tile roof.

In the distance, other similar homes dotted the steep hills on either side, but Alan's home, far enough below the road to be shielded from the curious eyes of passers-by, had a feeling of complete privacy. The endless glittering sea stretched out to the horizon, and Brooke was sure that from the rear of the house one would probably have an even better view of that great expanse. Her eyes sparkling with pleasure, she turned to her companion.

"Alan, this is gorgeous! I feel like I'm on a movie set! Is all this real?"

"Very much so," he smiled indulgently, apparently enjoying her delight. "I hope you'll feel at home here until you've regained your strength." He alighted from the car in one lithe movement and a moment later was opening her door and helping her out.

"Here we are," he said, handing her the crutches from the trunk. "Do you think you can manage by—what's wrong, Brooke?"

Feeling light-headed when she stood, Brooke clutched dizzily at the car.

"I—I don't know." She put a hand to her forehead and frowned. "I feel a little dizzy. I guess I'm more tired than I thought."

Abruptly she felt herself being swept up into two strong arms, and she clung gratefully to his neck and closed her eyes.

"I'm sorry," she murmured. "Nothing like this has ever happened to me before."

"You've probably never had a concussion or a badly

50

wrenched knee before, either," he reminded her. "Perhaps we should call the doctor."

"Oh, no, I'll be fine. I think I just need to lie down for awhile," she said. "Actually, I feel better already. I think I can make it on my own now."

Instead of putting her down, however, Alan began walking toward the house. She was about to protest, but when she noted the uncompromising line of his jaw, her objection died on her lips. It would do no good to argue that she was too heavy. He had swung her up as if she weighed no more than a feather, and he was now striding as easily and purposefully toward the house as if he were carrying no more than a briefcase.

She was more aware of his masculinity now than ever before, and she was almost frightened by the overwhelming physical attraction she felt for him. She'd never experienced anything like it before. She could hear the frantic drumming of her pulses, but she was pressed so tightly against his hard chest that she couldn't be sure if it were her own heart beating or his.

She wondered if Alan had any suspicion of the storm of emotion that engulfed her, but when she glanced up at him his face was an unreadable mask. Did he ever lose control? There was no time to speculate, however, for the door ahead of them swung open immediately by a thin gray-haired woman.

"Is this the poor child?" she asked in heavily accented English, standing aside to let Alan pass.

"Yes. Brooke, this is Suzanne, my housekeeper and cook—the one most responsible for keeping this house running smoothly. Suzanne, this is Miss Peyton."

"It's nice to meet you, Suzanne." Brooke smiled self-consciously. She'd never been introduced to anyone before while being held in a man's arms. But if Suzanne saw anything unusual in the situation, she didn't show it. Perhaps, if Alan's reputation were true, Suzanne had seen much stranger things, Brooke surmised.

"My pleasure, mademoiselle."

"Is Miss Peyton's room ready, Suzanne? She's rather tired and I know she would like to get some rest."

"Of course. I have prepared the green room, as you requested."

"Fine. Miss Peyton's things are in the car. Would you ask Jacques to bring them in, please?"

"Immediately," she replied.

Alan carried her through the multi-leveled house quickly, so Brooke had only a fleeting impression of deep carpets, rich furnishings, and vast expanses of glass on the sea-side of the house. Through the windows she glimpsed a stone terrace and lush vegetation. She longed for a closer look, but they soon entered a hall, and Alan stopped at a half-open door.

"This will be your home for the next few days," he told her as he pushed the door fully open with his shoulder. "I hope you'll be comfortable here."

As he carefully set her down in a deeply cushioned chair that was upholstered in a bright green and white tropical fabric, she gazed about in delight. The room was decorated with colors that made it seem an extension of the outdoors. Green predominated—on the bedspread and drapes, which matched the chair, and in the rug. Touches of sky blue and sunshine yellow added striking accents to the room. A dressing table with a lighted mirror stood in an adjacent bath/dressing room. One wall of the room was composed almost entirely of glass, and sliding doors led to a small balcony which contained two wrought iron chairs and a tiny table. The balcony seemed to jut out over a chasm, but Brooke couldn't see far enough down to tell for sure from where she sat. The view was magnificent.

"This is beautiful!" she exclaimed, turning to Alan with shining eyes.

"I'm glad you're pleased." He smiled, and she thought she detected a note of satisfaction in his voice.

There was a soft knock on the door and Alan stepped aside to let a slender, gray-haired man enter. His twinkling eyes looked at Brooke curiously.

"Brooke, this is Jacques, the gardener, general handyman, and sometimes-chauffeur. Without him and Suzanne, I don't know what I'd do. Jacques, this is Miss Peyton."

"How do you do?" he murmured in careful English, with a shy smile and a slight bow.

"It's nice to meet you, Jacques," Brooke said, returning the smile. "I haven't seen much of the grounds yet, but from the little sample I've had I would say I'm in for a treat."

"Thank you, mademoiselle." He smiled with pleasure. Then he turned to Alan. "Where would you like these?" he asked, indicating the boxes he was carrying.

"Brooke?" Alan turned to her.

"Oh." She glanced quickly around the room. "I guess over there," she said, indicating a love seat against the far wall. Jacques deposited them silently and then left.

"I know you need to rest, but wouldn't you like some lunch first?" Alan asked.

"To be honest, the only thing that looks good to me right now is that bed," she said ruefully, and then stopped short. Was that a suggestive remark? Then she gave herself a mental shake. She couldn't spend the next few days worrying about every remark she made. It was an innocent comment, and Alan seemed to have taken it as such, for his face didn't change expression.

"Normally I would argue with you. I know you haven't eaten since morning. But I think you're right. You look like you need rest more than food. But we'll make up for it at dinner. I'll find Suzanne and send her in to help you change."

"I'm sure I can manage," she said.

He turned at the door to give her one of his enigmatic smiles.

"Don't always be so independent, Brooke. There's nothing wrong with accepting some help once in a while. Enjoy being pampered while you have the chance."

"You win. I'm just used to doing things for myself."

His dark eyes bored into hers, and he seemed on the verge of making a remark about her statement.

"I'll send Suzanne in. Have a good rest," he replied instead.

"I'm sure I will."

A few minutes later, after Suzanne had helped her change, closed the drapes, and departed quietly, Brooke lay staring at the ceiling. How could she possibly waste time sleeping? She wanted to enjoy every moment of her stay here. Mary would never believe it!

But despite herself, Brooke soon found her eyes growing heavy, and within minutes she was asleep, oblivious to her elegant surroundings.

## Chapter Five

Brooke was standing in the middle of a street and a dark object was bearing down on her. She tried to run, but her feet wouldn't move. Something heavy was holding them in place, and she grew panicky. In a few moments the object would hit her, for it was almost upon her. She had to get out of the way! She had to...

With a strangled cry, Brooke's eyes flew open and she sat up abruptly, gazing about, disoriented, at the dim outline of the objects in the room in which she lay. She sighed shakily and closed her eyes. It had only been a nightmare!

Gradually, as her heart rate slowed, she realized that she must have slept for quite some time. She glanced at her watch—one of the few things that had survived the accident intact—but, with the shades drawn, it was too dark to read the face. She reached over and flipped on the bedside lamp. To her horror she saw that it was seven o'clock. She had slept for almost six hours! Why had no one awakened her?

Gingerly she eased her leg off the bed and reached for the crutches. As she rose there was a soft knock on the door. "Yes?" she called.

"It is Suzanne. I saw your light and wondered if I might be of some help."

"Oh, yes. Come in." Brooke was going to take Alan's

advice and enjoy being pampered—at least until she was better able to maneuver on her own.

"Shall I hang up all of your new things first?" Suzanne inquired, nodding toward the boxes on the couch.

"Yes, that would be fine. I hope I haven't kept dinner waiting," Brooke said anxiously.

"Oh, no. Monsieur d'Aprix never dines until eight or eight-thirty. You have plenty of time to get ready," the woman assured her.

"Good," Brooke said with a sigh of relief. "I wouldn't want to have anyone going hungry on my account."

"I am sure Monsieur d'Aprix would not have minded waiting," Suzanne said diplomatically. "Would you like to freshen up while I get your clothes ready?"

"Yes, thank you." Brooke gathered up her makeup and other toilet articles and made her way toward the bath. It, too, was decorated in shades of green, and she cast an admiring gaze on the green marble sink and sunken tub. A quick wash would have to suffice tonight.

When she emerged a few minutes later, Suzanne looked at her in surprise.

"Are these all your things, Mademoiselle Peyton?"

"Yes. I'll only be staying a few days."

"I see," the woman replied discreetly. "I didn't know what you would like to wear this evening, but I took the liberty of laying something out for you. If you wish to wear a different ensemble, I will be happy to get it out for you."

"No, this is fine," Brooke said. Actually, she was glad for Suzanne's initiative because she hadn't known whether Alan dressed for dinner. Apparently it was an informal meal, for Suzanne had chosen a pastel blue gored skirt and a simple peasant-style blouse with embroidery that Madame Barry had assured Brooke was most flattering to her.

56

A few minutes later, as she gazed at her reflection in the mirror, Brooke had to admit that the woman had been right. The outfit suited her perfectly, giving her an appealing air of innocence and youth.

"You look most charming," Suzanne said approvingly. "Monsieur d'Aprix said that he would meet you on the terrace whenever you are ready."

"Thank you. I'll be down in a few minutes."

"Très bien, mademoiselle." Suzanne left, closing the door softly behind her.

Brooke glanced at her watch. It was just past seven forty-five and she knew she should go down to the terrace, but first she wanted to see the view from the balcony outside her room. The glass door slid open easily and silently at her touch. It was just growing dusk, and the few boats visible in the distance had turned on their lights. A cool breeze lifted her hair away from her face, and at the shoreline below she could see the foaming surf crashing against the rocks.

The drop-off from her balcony wasn't as sharp as she'd thought earlier. Her room was located at one end of the curving house. From this position she had a good view of the entire structure, whose several levels clung to the cliffs in a U-shape. Below her was the terrace, sheltered on three sides by the house, with a short wall topped with flower boxes on the fourth. A small gate and several steps led from the terrace to the level below, which featured a large swimming pool surrounded by attractive lawn furniture. Below that was a well-tended garden.

A sudden movement diverted Brooke's attention from the garden back to the terrace. Alan had stepped out of the house and was moving casually toward the wall of the terrace, a drink in one hand and his other hand in the pocket of his slacks, a gesture that was becoming familiar to Brooke. He paused at the edge of the terrace and stared pensively out toward the sea, occasionally taking sips of his drink.

Brooke felt almost like an intruder as she watched him. But she couldn't help herself. Nor could she prevent the heavy thudding that had begun in her chest and the tingles of excitement that ran down her spine.

Was she becoming infatuated with Alan d'Aprix? She chided herself for being fanciful. Her reactions could be explained by the fact that she'd never met anyone before who could be called a playboy or a jet-setter. She was out of her element, in a world about which she'd only read, and it was natural to be excited. There was nothing more to it than that, she told herself firmly.

Still, as she stared down at Alan's tall form, clad in brown slacks and a cream-colored jacket with an open-necked shirt, she trembled slightly. She must maintain more control of her emotions or he would think her no more than a silly schoolgirl.

Resolutely she stepped back inside and slid the glass door shut, pausing a moment at the mirror to give her appearance one last check. She'd washed her hair and brushed it until it shone, and her darkly fringed eyes looked even larger than normal.

Her delicately tinted lips curved up in a faint smile. She might nót be in the same class with the other women in Alan's life, but no one could find fault with her appearance. She had been blessed with good looks of the sweet rather than dramatic type, and that was fine with her.

Carefully Brooke opened the door of her room and made her way down the hall. She caught glimpses of sparkling crystal and the satiny sheen of fine wood in the dining room before she emerged into the drawing room, which was decorated in the muted shades of asters—pink, purple, lavender-blue, and lavender with touches of green.

*Understated elegance*, she decided approvingly. A fireplace with a white marble mantel was flanked by two couches in an exquisite print, and various chairs in accent colors were artfully arranged around the room on a sky-blue carpet. Despite its elegance, it was invitingly comfortable, and Brooke sighed with pleasure. What must it be like to live—permanently—in a place like this?

With a last lingering glance, she made her way toward the French doors that led to the terrace, pausing to fumble with the catch while she tried to balance on the crutches. Almost immediately the doors were opened from the other side, and Alan smiled down at her.

"Can I give you a hand?" he asked.

"You just did." She smiled. "I thought I was going to have to eat my dinner on this side of the doors."

"I wouldn't have permitted that." He stepped aside to allow her out.

The light banter put Brooke at ease, and she found her tenseness evaporating.

"I hope I haven't kept you waiting," she said.

"Not at all. I don't usually dine before eight when I'm in France. Americans eat so early that I find I have to readjust my eating schedule every time I go back and forth."

He seated her at a low table with two chairs turned slightly toward one another for conversation, but the sweeping view of the sea was clearly visible.

"That's a most becoming outfit," he said as he casually sat across from her, leaned back and crossed his long legs.

"Thank you. Madame Barry suggested it. She was very helpful."

"I thought she would be," he nodded in satisfaction. "Mother shops there whenever she visits. Her taste is impeccable, and she has a great deal of confidence in Madame Barry."

So that was why Alan knew the store owner! His mother shopped there! She'd assumed…well, what

59

did it matter? But for some irrational reason her heart suddenly felt lighter.

"Now, Brooke, you must tell me something about yourself since I've already told you my life story."

He had hardly done that, and Brooke intended only to give a very brief account of her life. But prodded by his interested questions, she found herself opening up. She talked of her parents, her schooling, her life in England, and she told him about Mrs. Bates and her wonderful bequest.

"I still can't believe that someone who was practically a stranger would be so generous," she said, awed again by the woman's gift. "And you have been wonderful, too," she added with simple honesty.

He looked across at her in the dim light of the terrace, but she couldn't see his face clearly.

"I have a feeling that you bring out the best in people, Brooke." Before she could reply to that unexpected compliment, he changed the subject. "Tell me about your plans now."

As she described her study in London and her hopes for work when she returned home, her natural enthusiasm animated her face. She was hardly aware of their move to the small dining table, and although she noted the food she was eating—chicken in a wine sauce, puffed potatoes, and asparagus with hollandaise sauce—she was only vaguely conscious of the delicious flavors.

She had never met any man to whom she could talk so openly. Most of the men of her acquaintance asked only enough questions to be polite, and often they didn't even pretend interest when she responded.

By the time the chocolate mousse arrived, Brooke realized that she had been talking steadily for more than an hour. Discreet lighting now softly illuminated the terrace, and the candles on the table had burned low.

"My goodness, why didn't you stop me!" she exclaimed when she glanced at her watch. "I've hardly given you a chance to say a word all evening. I don't know what came over me. I don't usually talk this much," she apologized. "You're a good listener."

"Not always," he admitted, shrugging aside her compliment. "But you're a very interesting person, Brooke. I've enjoyed hearing about your life."

Brooke was inordinately pleased that Alan d'Aprix—financier, playboy, tycoon—found her enjoyable to be with. She would never have guessed that someone with his experience would take pleasure in her company.

"But I'm afraid I didn't give you a chance to say much." She apologized again, trying to keep her voice from betraying her pleasure at his compliment.

"I'll make up for it another time," he promised. "Would you like to sit on the terrace for a while?"

They sat in companionable silence for some time, watching the moon rising over the sea and chatting about inconsequential things. At last Alan turned to her.

"I know the accident has interrupted your holiday, so I thought while you're here you might enjoy seeing some of the surrounding country. I'll be busy a great deal of the time, of course, but I thought we might squeeze in a few outings. Would you like that?"

"Oh, yes!" she replied enthusiastically. Then her eyes clouded. "But I don't want to take you away from your work. I'm sure I've disrupted many of your plans already."

"Indeed you have," he said so softly that she glanced up, wondering if she'd imagined it. But he was busily helping her to her feet and skillfully guiding her toward the door. He continued speaking as if nothing else had been said.

"Why don't you plan to rest tomorrow? Get up whenever you like, spend some time by the pool, and we'll have dinner about the same time. I'll be tied up with business all day, but perhaps the day after we can do some sightseeing."

"That sounds fine," she agreed. They were inside now, and he turned to her.

"Can you make it back to your room?"

"Oh, yes. I'm getting quite good with these," she said, indicating the crutches with a nod.

"Pretty soon you won't need any help at all," he said, smiling slightly. "Well, have a good sleep. I'll see you tomorrow."

She turned and started down the hall. When she reached the corner she glanced back and was surprised to find Alan staring at her, his eyes brooding. What was he thinking?

But as he realized she was looking back at him, the pensive expression left his face and he raised his hand.

"Good night," he called. Then he was gone, disappearing into the shadows of the hall on the other side of the drawing room.

## Chapter Six

Brooke slept well, with no recurrence of the nightmare that had plagued her nap the previous afternoon. When she awoke the sun was trying to push its way through the cracks in the drapes, and a glance at her watch told her it was nine o'clock.

With a contented sigh, she snuggled under the covers and stared at the ceiling. Mary would never believe this. It was all too much like a dream. In fact, she ought to pinch herself to make sure she wasn't really asleep. But no, she was wide awake. It was all real. If nothing else, the elastic bandage on her knee told her that.

Carefully she eased her leg off the bed and stood up. Her knee felt much better today, she noted, as she tested her weight on it gently. Too bad she had to wear that ugly bandage. But without it she would never have met Alan d'Aprix or had the chance to stay in a magnificent villa or had beautiful new clothes or…she laughed softly to herself. Now that was looking on the bright side of things! Mrs. Bates would have approved of her attitude, she thought with a grin.

She dressed leisurely in a pair of beige slacks and an off-white tunic top with a wide brown leather belt. Alan had told her to relax and take her time doing things today, and she intended to follow his orders. But in general she felt much improved. The persistent headache from the concussion had all but disappeared and she felt very rested. Nevertheless, it would be nice to have a day just to loaf.

This time as she made her way down the hall she took time to examine her surroundings in more detail. Her previous impressions were confirmed. *Elegant. Expensive. Understated.* Those were the words that came to mind immediately.

Many of the doors along the hall were shut, and Brooke assumed they were guest bedrooms. A formal dining room, with a gleaming crystal chandelier, caused her to pause in admiration for a few moments before she continued toward the drawing room. As she entered, she glanced curiously in the direction in which Alan had disappeared the night before and wondered if that wing of the house was his private suite. As if in answer to her question, Suzanne appeared from another doorway and, seeing the direction of Brooke's gaze, spoke.

"Those are Monsieur d'Aprix's private rooms. He allows no one to enter there," she explained. "It is his— how you say?—retreat. A place where he can be alone."

"Everyone needs a spot like that," Brooke said, smiling. "The whole house is lovely. You must enjoy living here."

"Oh, yes. Monsieur d'Aprix is a wonderful employer. Jacques and I have been with him since he built this home. Would you like some breakfast now, Mademoiselle Peyton?"

"I am a bit hungry," Brooke admitted. "But please don't go to any trouble."

"It is no trouble," Suzanne said. "Monsieur d'Aprix said you were to eat a big breakfast."

*Another example of Alan's sometimes imperious manner,* Brooke noted. But somehow she, who had always liked being independent and making her own decisions, didn't mind. Maybe it was because she

64

could never argue with his judgment. It always seemed flawless.

"Would you like to wait on the terrace?" Suzanne suggested.

Brooke did just that, relishing the gentle breeze, the colorful vegetation, and the silence, interrupted only occasionally by the call of the birds. The breakers were too far away to be heard, but Brooke could imagine the sound as they crashed on the distant rocks.

When Alan had ordered a big breakfast, he had meant it quite literally. Suzanne brought a full tray to the glass-topped table. Bacon, eggs, potatoes, and the ever-present flaky, melt-in-the-mouth croissants and jam, as well as a steaming cup of cocoa, were arrayed on the tray.

"I'll never be able to finish all that!" exclaimed Brooke as Suzanne arranged the dishes on the table. But a short time later, as she surveyed the empty plates, she grinned. She had been hungrier than she'd thought. As Suzanne cleared the table she smiled at Brooke.

"I know you will not be able to swim, but you might enjoy getting some sun down by the pool. Would you like me to ask Jacques to help you down the steps?"

"I'm sure I can make it. And that sounds like a marvelous idea! I had planned to spend some time on the beach while I was on the Riviera, and this is just as good. Even better, in fact, because it's so secluded."

Back in her room, Brooke donned the emerald green swimsuit she had purchased at Madame Barry's urging. She had thought she would have no use for it. Now, as she looked in the mirror, she was glad she had relented. It was a one-piece suit, with a deeply plunging neckline and spaghetti straps that crisscrossed in the back. It revealed her well-proportioned figure to perfection. She added a short terry cloth cover-up, and within a few minutes she was stretched luxuriously in a chaise lounge by the pool. This was the life!

She read all morning from a book selected from Alan's well-stocked library, but she frequently glanced up to assure herself that she was actually at a villa on the Riviera. Each time she did so, a small smile curved her lips gracefully, and it was at just such a moment that Alan appeared. When she noticed him silently staring at her from the bottom of the steps she jumped visibly.

"I'm sorry if I startled you," he apologized as he came toward her. "I was just pausing a moment to enjoy the view."

Brooke gave him a suspicious look, but if he had meant the remark suggestively his face did not give him away.

"It is lovely here," she replied. Suddenly aware of her scanty attire, she reached instinctively for her robe.

"Had enough sun?" Alan inquired casually.

"I think so," she replied, trying to match his casual tone as she self-consciously slipped into the cover-up. "I burn easily."

"I believe that. You're very fair. How does the knee feel today?"

"Much better, thanks. I may not even need those much longer," she said nodding toward the crutches.

"I'm sure you won't be sorry about that," he said, smiling. "Have you eaten lunch?"

"After that enormous breakfast? You must be joking!"

"Well, suppose I take a quick swim and we have lunch here by the pool?"

"That would be fine. But I'll have to stick to something light."

"How about a salad? I always try to eat lightly at lunch, too."

"Sounds good."

"I'll let Suzanne know and then I'll change and join you."

When he reappeared in navy blue swim trunks, a towel around his neck, and wearing dark glasses, Brooke caught her breath. He was darkly tanned, and while he was not overly muscular, it was obvious that he was in excellent physical condition. There was not an ounce of excess weight on his lean body. He walked toward her and deposited his towel and glasses on a chair.

"I wish you could join me. I'm sure that must be a nuisance," he said, nodding toward the bandage.

"I'm getting used to it," Brooke shrugged. "That water does look inviting, though," she added wistfully. Then she brightened. "But I'm enjoying myself, anyway."

"You always seem to make the best of every situation. I admire that, Brooke," he told her. "Most women would want to be waited on hand and foot if they were in your condition."

"I haven't been here long," she said lightly. "Wait until I've been around a few days. I may get very demanding."

"I doubt that."

She watched him dive gracefully into the pool, noting the strong, clean strokes that pulled him powerfully through the water as he swam. She had to admit that she was physically attracted to him as she had never been attracted to any man before. Sometimes the power of that attraction frightened her, and she wondered if, given certain circumstances, she would be able to hold her emotions in check. She hoped she would never be put to the test. But at the same time, she found herself longing to know what it would be like to be held in his strong arms, to feel his mouth on hers, to hear the hammering of his heart as he pressed her close....

"That was very refreshing."

Brooke looked up, startled. Alan had emerged glistening from the water and was toweling himself dry.

She stared up at him and blushed. Could he possibly know what she had been thinking? *Of course not*, she told herself impatiently, but her cheeks burned nonetheless and she looked away for a moment. When she turned back, Suzanne was coming down the steps with a tray. She placed two large plates of salad on the table, along with a basket of crusty French bread and two glasses of iced tea.

"Will there be anything else, Monsieur d'Aprix?" she inquired.

"No thanks, Suzanne."

As they began to eat, he asked whether she liked the book she had chosen from the library. This led to a discussion of literature in general, and Brooke quickly discovered that he had read widely and that their tastes were similar. In fact they had both recently re-read *A Tale of Two Cities*. When at last he rose—was there a reluctance in his manner, or was it simply wishful thinking on her part?—she couldn't believe the time had gone by so quickly.

"I'm afraid I'll have to get back. But I'll see you about eight for dinner. Is there anything you need?"

"No. What more could a person want? It's perfect here."

"I'm glad you're enjoying it. Have a nice afternoon." With a wave he was gone.

Brooke not only had a nice afternoon, she also had a nice evening and a nice week. Alan arranged a sightseeing trip of some sort almost every afternoon or evening—the palace and casino at Monte Carlo, the flower market at Nice, and other picturesque spots. One day they dined in a quaint inn overlooking the sea, and Brooke thought she was in heaven. It was too perfect to last.

Later that week, after a visit to Dr. Lafitte during which he pronounced her ready to travel, she knew that her adventure was almost over. She sat in the doctor's waiting room while Alan talked with the physician, aimlessly paging through a French magazine. She could read very little of it, but it didn't matter. Though her eyes were on the page, her thoughts were elsewhere. The knowledge that she would soon be leaving caused a slightly sick feeling in the pit of her stomach, and she was overcome with an emptiness she couldn't explain.

It was more than the fact that she would miss the luxury and pampering. It was Alan himself. She might as well admit it, though she had never seriously believed that people could fall in love so quickly. She knew that in Alan she had found the man she had always dreamed of. He was tender, but strong; gentle, but masculine. He was considerate, generous, and intelligent. Intuitively she knew that he was also deeply principled and honorable, the kind of man who would respect the woman he loved and work to achieve that spiritual union she so longed to have.

An image from the past flashed into her mind. She was seven years old and her parents had taken her to a carnival, where she had eagerly climbed into the seat of the Ferris wheel for her first ride. But as the giant wheel began to turn, she became frightened. Her father had reached over with a smile and taken her hand.

"Don't be afraid, Brooke."

And suddenly she hadn't been. Instead, she had enjoyed the sweeping exhilaration of the ride because she had shared it with someone she loved and trusted. Life with Alan would be like that, she thought, daily sharing that same exhilaration.

But the love was only on her side, she reminded herself sharply. Though she desperately longed to see some sign of his returned affection, she'd known from the beginning that his kindness was only that, nothing more. He was merely being hospitable out of a sense of responsibility. How could he love someone as unsophisticated as she was?

The longer she sat there, the bleaker she felt. But at

last she realized that if Alan came out and saw her dejection, he would know that something was wrong. He might even guess her feelings, and she didn't want that. He had done nothing to encourage her. True to his word, he had not attempted to be anything more than a concerned friend. He had not touched her except to help her when she couldn't manage on her own. So anything she felt was her own fault.

The door to the inner office opened and Brooke looked up, forcing a cheerful expression onto her face.

"I'm as good as new, right?" she said, a little too brightly.

"Well, I would not go that far." Dr. Lafitte smiled. "But yes, you are much better. You won't need the crutches anymore, and you may travel if you wish. Your own doctor will be able to take care of you now. The bandage can come off in another week or so."

"Thank you, doctor. You've been very kind."

He gave a slight bow. Alan spoke to him in low tones for a moment, and then he turned toward Brooke.

"Ready to go home?"

She nodded. *If only it were her home!*

She was unusually silent on the drive back, and finally Alan turned to her.

"Is something wrong, Brooke?"

"No, of course not. I was just making plans. There are a lot of details to attend to," she lied. "I guess I should start making the arrangements to return to England."

"Not today, though. It's late."

"At least I can start packing my things," she replied. She looked up at him in time to see his jaw tighten. When he spoke, though, his voice was light and casual. "Why not worry about that tomorrow? Tonight we'll have a nice dinner on the terrace and just relax."

Brooke agreed readily. What harm could there be in putting off her departure preparations one more day?

He smiled down at her, and her heart once more began to hammer as his dark eyes met hers. "I have some work to finish," he glanced at his watch, "so why don't I meet you on the terrace about seven-thirty?"

When Brooke appeared at the appointed time, dressed in a white sundress with blue trim that revealed a large expanse of her now golden skin, Alan was already waiting for her. He rose when he saw her at the doorway.

"You look lovely tonight, Brooke." He smiled at her as she seated herself.

"Thank you," she replied, a small smile playing at her lips. Why did this man make her feel so special when he looked at her? If only she hadn't come to care about him so deeply!

Over a dinner of beef burgundy, green beans almondine, crisp salad, and more of the delicious crusty bread, they chatted amiably. Alan had taken to relating amusing anecdotes to her of his day's activities, and Brooke frequently found herself laughing during the meal despite the fact that there was a sinking feeling in the pit of her stomach at the prospect of leaving. Alan didn't refer to her upcoming departure, so Brooke avoided the subject also. But when dessert arrived—a chocolate souffle´—she let a remark slip.

"Oh, that's beautiful!" she exclaimed in delight as Suzanne, beaming at the compliment, placed the dessert on the table and began to serve it. "Maybe it's a good thing that I'll be leaving soon. If I ate like this all the time, I'd have a real weight problem."

Although Alan continued to smile she saw his eyes narrow, and she wondered what she had said to displease him. Could he, too, be reluctant that she was leaving? But no, if anything he'd be glad to be rid of her, for she had certainly disrupted his life. Several times after he'd taken her on outings she had seen his light burning late, so he obviously had to catch up on his work in the evenings. Although he had never been anything but gracious to her, she would have thought he'd be glad to dispose of his obligation to her.

She looked at him surreptitiously as she spooned the creamy chocolate confection into her mouth. He seemed lost in thought, a slight frown on his forehead. Suddenly he glanced up and caught her looking at him.

"This is delicious," she remarked, quickly lowering her eyes.

"Yes, isn't it? Suzanne is an excellent cook. I look forward to her meals when I'm here." He replaced his napkin on the table and looked at her questioningly. "Shall we have our coffee on the terrace?"

Brooke nodded her assent, and soon they were seated in deeply cushioned deck chairs. For a time they sat in silence, enjoying the dark quiet of the sea and the shimmering, ethereal quality of the light from the full moon on its surface. In the distance a few lights on boats were visible, and a gentle breeze blew in the sheltered area of the terrace. With a contented sigh, Brooke relaxed even more deeply in her chair. Alan looked over at her, and though it was difficult to see his face clearly in the dim light, she detected a smile in his voice.

"Happy?"

"Mmmm," she murmured.

"I hope your stay has been a pleasant one, Brooke. At least as pleasant as possible, considering your injuries."

"Oh, it has! I've enjoyed myself so much! I felt like a real lady of leisure. Late breakfasts, sunning by the pool all day, private tours of the area by a very capable guide, delicious food...what more could a woman ask?"

"I'm glad to hear that our hospitality was satisfactory," he said teasingly in response to her praise.

" 'Satisfactory' hardly does justice to your kindness," she said quietly, her voice now serious. "I can't thank you enough, Alan. You've more than made up

72

for the injuries—which were at least half my fault, anyway. I really feel I owe *you* something. I know the
chances are slim that you'd ever need anything from
me, but if ever I can do anything for you in return,
please don't hesitate to ask."

"Do you really mean that, Brooke?" Alan asked, his
tone now as serious as hers.

"Of course," she replied in surprise. Was he going to
take her up on her offer? What could she do for him?

"Then there is one favor I'd like to ask." He paused
as if trying to decide whether to proceed with his request. Puzzled, Brooke leaned forward, a frown on her
forehead. She waited in silence, her curiosity building.
Finally he put down his coffee cup and turned to her,
but the shadows on his face hid the expression in his
eyes. He drew in his breath slowly before he spoke.

"Would you marry me, Brooke?"

# Chapter Seven

In the few moments of silence that followed, Brooke was aware only of the pounding of her heart. Her throat constricted and she was having trouble breathing. Could she possibly have heard him correctly, or were her ears playing tricks on her? She turned to stare at him in the darkness, her hand at her throat.

He was looking at her, and although his face was still in shadows, she could feel the intense, piercing gaze of his eyes through the blackness. She could sense his rigid attention while he waited for her reply. Surely this was a dream, a product of her sometimes overactive imagination. Yet, if that was the case, why was he staring at her like that?

"Did...did you just ask me to marry you?" she whispered incredulously.

"Yes." He reached over to take her hand. A delicious tingle ran through her at his touch, and she had to force herself to pay attention to his next words. "I know this is a shock," he admitted, his tone serious but warm. "And I know it's a big favor to ask. But it would help me out of a rather difficult situation."

"What do you mean?"

"I'm currently involved in negotiations with a shipping tycoon by the name of Nicholas Pappas, who owns a prime piece of property in Greece that I'm interested in acquiring for a new hotel," he explained.

"Things were looking promising until a complication—in the form of Nick's daughter, Daphne—arose. Unfortunately, she's become rather...taken...with me, and Nick is interested in encouraging the match. In fact, he's intimated that the closing of the deal may rest on whether another—more personal—deal is also closed.

"I have no interest in Daphne beyond the fact that she is the daughter of a business acquaintance," he said with a shrug. "Nick is basically a fair man, and although Daphne is able more or less to wrap him around her finger, I know he wouldn't continue to make the sale contingent on a development of our relationship if I were married. So now you can see why it would be a great help to me if you would agree to be my wife."

Throughout his speech Alan's tone, while pleasant, had been very businesslike and straightforward. Brooke's heart sank. What a fool she was! How could she expect someone like Alan d'Aprix to be romantically interested in her when he could have his pick of rich and beautiful women?

"This would be strictly a business arrangement," Alan assured her when she didn't respond. "And only for a limited time, of course. We can have the marriage annulled quietly when I've concluded my business. There would be no obligations on your part during the marriage except to appear with me at social functions and act as a hostess in my home. I'll provide a generous allowance after the annulment, of course, that will keep you free from financial worries for some time."

Brooke stared at him in the darkness, glad that he couldn't read the expression in her eyes. She felt stung. How could he be so crass about marriage, treating it completely as a business deal, especially after what he had said about his own parents' divorce?

Brooke had thought he felt the same way she did about marriage—that it was a sharing, loving partner-

76

ship between two people who truly cared about one another and had committed themselves to each other for a lifetime.

"But Alan, I thought you said that when you married you wanted it to last for your whole life," she said, hardly able to control the surge of emotion she felt churning in her stomach.

"I do," he replied promptly, and then added quietly, "but of course I meant that in terms of my real marriage." He emphasized the word *real*.

"I see." But she didn't. To make marriage into a business deal was to diminish its sacredness and destroy its meaning. She wasn't so naive as to think marriages weren't sometimes arranged in this manner—and had been throughout history—but she had never imagined being faced with that prospect herself. To her it was a violation of the sanctity of the institution.

If only Alan had not been so terribly kind! That kindness, and the sense of honor she had come to associate with him, now haunted her thoughts. She had no reason to believe the respect he had shown her all week had been false. Perhaps now, too, there was nothing amiss in his proposal—after all, his judgments always seemed so flawless.

It wouldn't, as he had pointed out, be a real marriage. In fact, she could look upon it as a job rather than a marriage. Then it wouldn't be so bad. But could she stand to be close to him every day, playing the part of a loving wife, all the while knowing that to him she was simply a "business associate"? The last thing she wanted was to reveal her love for him, for then he would feel guilty, and she loved him too much to put that burden on him.

"Is this really fair to Mr. Pappas?" she asked, trying to stall for time while she put her thoughts in order.

"In the long run he'll thank me," Alan said with a shrug. "It's a profitable deal for both of us, and he's just letting his daughter sway his normally sound judgment. If he canceled the deal because of her he'd end up regretting it. I'm actually doing him a favor by removing this obstacle to the transaction."

"But won't people think it strange if you suddenly marry someone you've only known a short time?"

Again he shrugged. "People are used to the eccentricities of the wealthy. Oh, I suppose there will be a few raised eyebrows. On the other hand, I'm at an age when many men in my position begin to think about a family."

"I see," she said again. He had obviously thought the whole thing through thoroughly. "And this would be strictly a business arrangement? And only for a short time?"

"Of course," he said quickly. "I realize what an imposition this is on you, Brooke. I know you're anxious to get back to the States, but I expect to have the deal wrapped up within a couple of months. And, as I said, there will be no...personal obligations."

Brooke shifted uncomfortably and looked over at him. It was clear that he had no interest in letting the relationship develop beyond a business agreement. She frowned and turned to look out toward the sea, torn by indecision. She wanted to be near him, but could she bear it, knowing that her love would never be returned? And could she hide her own feelings from him? Could her emotions pay the price?

"I know all of this is quite a shock, Brooke." Alan's voice was warm and sympathetic. "I don't expect you to give me an answer tonight. Why don't you think about it for a day or two and then let me know what you decide? I know I'm asking a lot, so if you feel that you don't want to take on the job, I'll understand. There won't be any hard feelings."

Brooke's heart melted. Why did he have to be so kind about it? He knew that she was wracked by doubts—although she was sure he didn't suspect her real feelings about him—and he had given her a way out by letting her know he realized the enormity of his request. Her heart ached with tenderness, and it was all she could do not to throw herself in his arms and tell him how much she loved him. How she would love to feel his arms about her, to feel his tender lips caressing hers! How wonderful it would be to be loved by this man, who she was sure would love with the same intensity as he lived. If only the proposal could have been for an authentic marriage!

With a deep, trembling sigh she rose to her feet. "You're right. I need to think about it," she said, hoping that her voice would not betray her turmoil.

"Of course. Good night, Brooke."

"Good night."

Though Brooke tried to put the events of the evening out of her mind, she found it impossible to fall asleep. At last she gave up, and with a sigh she got up and made her way out to the balcony. She stood in the darkness for some time before she noticed that Alan was still on the terrace below, his figure a dim outline in the moonlight. Apparently he, too, was finding sleep elusive.

With a puzzled frown she rested an elbow on the wrought iron railing of the balcony, cupped her chin in her hand and gazed down at him. Though his request had been businesslike and his explanation straightforward, there were nagging questions in her mind.

For one thing, if he needed a wife, why didn't he just ask one of the countless women she was sure would eagerly jump at the chance? After all, he had only known her a short time, and she was from a far different stratum of society than he. Wouldn't his friends and associates think it strange for him to marry someone with her background?

Still, Alan did not strike her as a man who did things without first thinking them through thoroughly. He must know what he was doing. The business deal he had mentioned sounded too important to take chances on. But she still didn't know why he had chosen her. The major question now, at least from a practical standpoint, was whether she could play the part well enough. No, she corrected herself, that wouldn't be the problem. She could give a convincing performance, but would she have the restraint to keep herself from overdoing it and thus reveal her true feelings? It would be so easy for her to slip—to forget that the marriage was not real—and thereby betray her love for him. That was something she would have to be on guard against constantly.

A movement below caught her eye, and she glanced down. Alan had risen and, hands in pockets, was slowly making his way toward the house. The moon silhouetted his muscular form. Perhaps he was already regretting the proposal. Or maybe he was just wondering what her answer would be.

*And what will it be?* she wondered, as he disappeared inside. The chance to spend more time with him was almost too tempting to pass up. On the other hand, if she stayed longer she knew she would fall more deeply in love, which would make the inevitable parting even more difficult. Was that pain worth the pleasure of staying a bit longer?

And most of all, could this mock marriage be justified on moral grounds? Would she be able to live with her conscience afterward? Or would the harm done outweigh the good acomplished? Her desire to repay Alan for his kindness, and, for that matter, just to be with him, played havoc with her long-held dreams of the sacred joy of a true marriage.

But perhaps she was taking the proposal too seriously. All parties would benefit, Alan had convinced her. And, ultimately, could he ever ask her to do anything truly wrong? It didn't seem possible.

Questions came readily, but the answers eluded her. Perhaps after a night's sleep she would be able to see things in better perspective. She quietly slipped back inside her room, closing the door behind her. Snuggled under the covers a few seconds later, she tried once again to turn her thoughts away from her decision. This time she was successful, and a few minutes later she was asleep.

Things did seem clearer when she woke up, for in her dreams a fragment of a conversation she'd had with her mother years before was replayed. As if her mother were actually with her again, Brooke could see her gentle smile and understanding eyes as they discussed a decision that Brooke had had to make about a close friend.

"You grew up with all the right values, Brooke," her mother had said. "Your father and I tried to instill them in you, but you deserve a great deal of credit for standing by them in this topsy-turvy world. I thank God every day that you have the kind of faith that will be a guiding force in your life. So always trust your heart, Brooke. It won't ever lead you wrong."

Brooke knew the next morning what her answer would be. Her heart told her to say yes. She would agree to Alan's proposal. He had been so kind to her, and he really wasn't asking that much—just her time, which she had in plentiful supply. No deep commitment was required of her, so, according to her definition, it wasn't a marriage in the real sense at all. Of course, she would have to keep her emotions under control. But somehow, in daylight, that didn't seem like such a difficult task.

She dressed hurriedly, quickly applying her makeup and running a brush through her hair. Now that she had decided to agree to the marriage, she wanted to tell Alan as soon as possible.

She gave herself a quick glance in the wall-length mirror, noticing with a grin the pale-beige skirt and the sheer beige and pale-green blouse tucked in at her slender waistline. It seemed an appropriate outfit in which to tell a man that you would marry him.

He was on the terrace, pensively gazing out to sea. Suddenly she felt shy and uncertain, but when he turned and she saw the haggard look on his face she summoned up her courage and gave him a tremulous smile.

"Good morning, Alan."

"Hello, Brooke. Did you sleep well?"

"So-so," she replied. "There was so much to think about."

"I know," he nodded, his eyes looking deeply into hers as if he were trying to discern her answer in their depths. She could feel the tension in the air. "Why don't we have some breakfast?" he suggested, stepping aside to let her pass.

"Alan," she reached out to him, touching his arm lightly. She took a deep breath, then smiled and spoke with confidence. "I've decided to accept your proposal."

An incredulous look came over his face, and then all the strain disappeared from his eyes and mouth. He took her hand and gave her a warm smile, his eyes suddenly alive.

"Are you sure?"

"Yes," she replied firmly. "You've done so much for me, this is the least I can do to repay you. I hope it helps you get the land you need."

For a moment he gave her a blank look. Then he smiled. "I'm sure it will. Well, we have quite a few things to attend to," he continued as he held the chair for her. "I'd like to have the marriage take place as soon as possible because I need to go to Paris on business next week. We can tell people that's our honeymoon."

Brooke's eyes grew wide. She hadn't thought of that. Alan caught her look and hastened to reassure her.

"Of course, it will be a honeymoon in name only. I'll be tied up most of the time with business. As I told you last night, Brooke, this is strictly a business arrangement. You don't have to worry about...it becoming more than that."

"I know," she nodded, keeping her eyes down. If

only he knew how much she wanted it to become more!

"I'll make all of the legal arrangements, but there are a few things we'll need to do together. Do you feel like going out today?"

"Yes, I feel fine. I've almost forgotten about this," she said, indicating her knee.

"Good," he nodded in satisfaction. While they ate he spoke of the tasks that needed to be accomplished before the wedding.

"First thing this morning we'll visit the jeweler and choose a ring."

"Is that really necessary?" Brooke interrupted him. When his eyes narrowed she quickly added, "I mean, it's for such a short time. I hate to see you go to any extra expense."

"You must have a ring," he stated firmly, and Brooke started to protest. "After all, everyone will expect it," he added, and he saw that this satisfied her. "Also, you'll need some more clothes."

Brooke was growing paler by the minute. A ring could be returned when the charade was over, but clothes were another story.

"But Alan, this is getting to be terribly expensive. Are you sure I need more clothes?"

"Yes, I'm sure, Brooke," he told her gently, taking her hand across the table. "Trust my judgment, okay? Believe me, this is a small investment, considering the return I'm hoping for."

"Okay, I guess you know best." She gave in with a smile.

"Now, as for the wedding itself—I thought a very small civil ceremony would be the most appropriate. What do you think?"

"That would be fine," she assured him. The less it seemed like her dream wedding—which included a church, flowers, bridesmaids, and a long white dress—the more she would be able to pretend that it was strictly business.

"I think everything is settled, then. Finished?" he asked as she placed her napkin back on the table.

"Yes."

"You didn't eat much," he remarked with a glance at her plate.

"I guess I'm too excited," she admitted. "It's not every day that a young woman gets married, after all," she tried to joke.

He smiled at her tenderly, and her heart ached with love.

"Things have moved a bit fast, haven't they? I imagine it's a bit overwhelming. You aren't sorry, are you? You can still call it off if you want to."

"No. I just need a little time to get used to the idea, that's all." With her hand in his warm clasp, everything seemed fine. She was confident that she had made the right decision.

"Good." He gave her hand a gentle squeeze before he released it. "I'll meet you in the foyer in fifteen minutes."

They rose to go into the house, and this time it was Alan who placed his hand on her arm. "I hope you realize how much I appreciate this, Brooke. I know I'm asking a lot, and I'm grateful."

"I'm glad I can help," she said sincerely. Their eyes met, and Brooke thought she detected an intensity of feeling in his that matched her own. But a moment later it was gone.

"See you in a few minutes," he said, removing his hand from her arm.

As they entered the quiet, deeply carpeted jeweler's shop, a short, slightly plump man came forward and greeted Alan cordially.

"I have put some pieces aside for you which I think will be most suitable," he said and then turned to Brooke. "And this is the bride-to-be, yes? Ah, your good fortune is the misfortune of every eligible gentleman in France," he said debonairly. "My congratulations to you both."

"Thank you, Alfred. Now, those rings..."

"Oui. I am sure you have many things to do. If you will come this way," he said, adeptly taking the cue and moving the subject to a less personal level. He led them into a small room that contained three chairs and a small table. The man ceremoniously spread a black velvet cloth on the table and then turned to them with a slight bow. "I will now get the rings."

"Alan, this looks like a terribly expensive place," Brooke whispered worriedly as the jeweler disappeared through the door. "Wouldn't a plain band of some sort do?"

Before Alan could respond, Alfred returned with a box. "I collected a few things after you called this morning. I think you will find something here to satisfy mademoiselle." With a flourish he spread the contents of the box before Brooke in a glittering array, and she gasped audibly at the sparkling gems.

"Ah! Mademoiselle is pleased," Alfred beamed in satisfaction.

"Oh, they're exquisite!" Brooke said in awe. Her eyes were drawn to a delicate gold band that was adorned by one large and several smaller diamonds. She picked it up reverently and examined it. Then, realizing the value of the gems spread before her, she quickly replaced it and turned to Alan, a look of panic in her eyes.

"I really don't know if I need something this elaborate," she said haltingly.

Alan took her hand before he spoke. With his eyes he seemed to be telling her to let him handle everything. Then he turned to the jeweler.

"We'll take that one," he said, indicating the ring Brooke had examined. She started to speak, but his hand tightened on hers and she stifled her protest.

"An excellent choice, Monsieur d'Aprix. This is a fine piece. Now let us see how it fits." The man started to reach for Brooke's hand, but Alan stopped him, took the ring, and placed it on her finger. Brooke stared at it numbly.

"That seems to be a perfect fit. How does it feel, mademoiselle?"

Brooke, her eyes still on the sparkling gems on her finger, forced herself to look up. "It's as if it were made for me," she said.

Alan rose and held her chair. "Thanks, Alfred. I'll have the bank draft sent to you Monday."

"There is no hurry, Monsieur d'Aprix." He turned to Brooke. "May I wish you both every happiness."

"Thank you," she murmured as Alan led her out the door. She was seated in the car before she could sufficiently collect her thoughts to speak again. "Alan, I can't accept this, even for a short time. I'm afraid I'll lose it. It's much too expensive."

"Do you like it, Brooke?"

She looked down at the exquisite ring and sighed. "I love it."

"Then enjoy it. I'll insure it, so don't worry about losing it."

"I guess you can return this when we…when your business deal is finished," she said. She saw him frown, but when he spoke his tone was conversational. "I do a fair amount of business with Alfred. I'm sure there will be no problem," he told her.

"Well, that makes me feel a little better," she admitted. "It is a beautiful ring, isn't it?" She watched in delight as the facets caught the morning sun. She turned to Alan and found him watching her.

"Yes, it is," he agreed, turning his attention back to the road. "You have very good taste, Brooke."

An illogical flood of warmth spread through her at his compliment, and she smiled to herself.

The next stop was Madame Barry's, and this time Brooke was left alone for a few minutes while Alan conferred with the owner. When they returned, he took her hand.

"I've explained the types of functions you'll be attending in the next few weeks, so Madame Barry will be able to suggest the appropriate clothes. You can rely on her judgment, Brooke." He turned back to the owner. "Please make sure my fiancee buys an ample amount of clothes. She has a tendency to be conservative."

He turned to smile at her tenderly. This time there was no mistaking the look in his eyes, and Brooke was astonished. He really was looking at her as a man would look at the woman he loved. Then, with a sinking feeling, she realized that it was an act for the benefit of the shop owner, just as his use of the word "fiancee" had been. She forced herself to smile in return, and before she could speak he leaned down and kissed her lightly. Her heart thumped heavily in her chest and she stared at him with wide eyes as he drew away.

"Have fun, dear," he said as he turned to go, and Brooke's heart melted at his use of the endearment. Her role might be harder to play than she had thought.

For the next few hours Brooke was kept busy viewing models, trying on dresses, and standing for fittings. Evening gowns, daytime dresses, sports clothes, swimsuits, cocktail dresses—she tried them all on. She occasionally protested that she didn't need so many things, but Madame Barry was firm.

"Monsieur d'Aprix said you were to have a full wardrobe, mademoiselle. And now we must choose some things for bedroom wear."

Brooke looked at the woman with a start. Had Alan specifically mentioned lingerie? But no, surely Madame Barry just naturally included it in her idea of a "full wardrobe." After all, it was an important part of a new bride's clothing.

Peignoir sets, each one more beautiful than the last, were brought out for her inspection, and Brooke smiled wistfully thinking to herself that only she would ever see them. They were obviously designed to please the opposite sex, so they would be wasted on her. Still, she had to act as if she were a bride-to-be, so she exclaimed over them appropriately and followed Madame Barry's suggestions in her selections.

When at last Brooke thought they were finished and sank back into her chair, Madame Barry pointed out that the most important item was yet to be chosen.

"What did I forget?" Brooke asked with a puzzled frown.

"Why, the wedding dress, of course!" the woman said in surprise.

"Oh, of course!" Brooke replied hastily. How stupid of her! Of course a bride would be interested in choosing a wedding dress. She hadn't actually planned to buy anything special, but perhaps Alan had told the woman otherwise. Still, she didn't want anything elaborate. That would make it seem too much like a real wedding.

"It's going to be a small wedding, you know," Brooke told the woman. "I just want something simple."

"I think we have just the thing." She motioned to a model waiting out of sight, and the girl advanced slowly into the room and executed a graceful turn. She wore a white dress with a simple scooped neckline that was edged with lace. The cap sleeves were made entirely of lace, and the hem of the wide skirt, which flared below a natural waistline, was also decorated with lace. It wasn't the wedding dress of her dreams, but it was nevertheless beautiful and perfect for the occasion.

"That will be just fine," Brooke said. "It's lovely."

As she fingered the lace, Brooke wished with all her heart that she was choosing a dress for a real wedding. But that was not to be. She would just have to accept the fact. But that didn't stop her from loving Alan, and she resolved to do everything in her power to help him as he had helped her.

## Chapter Eight

By the time Alan arrived back at the shop, Brooke was exhausted. She gave him a welcoming smile. "Am I glad to see you! Spending money is tiring," she complained good-naturedly.

"But enjoyable, I hope."

"Very. I've never seen so many beautiful clothes in all my life."

"I hope you got everything you needed," he said, with a meaningful glance at Madame Barry.

"This time, yes," the woman assured him.

"Good. Ready, Brooke?" He turned to her with a smile, and she nodded, basking in the warmth of his gaze. Even though she knew much of it was for the benefit of Madame Barry, she couldn't help but revel in his attention. With his hand resting lightly but possessively on her waist they left the exclusive shop.

The next few days were a whirlwind of activity. There were papers to be signed, packing to be supervised, and a visit to the doctor, who pronounced her knee almost back to normal.

Ever since the accident, Brooke had occasionally been plagued with the nightmare of a vehicle bearing down on her in the darkness. She always awoke just before it struck, sometimes sitting bolt upright in bed, her body clammy. But when the day of her wedding dawned, Brooke awoke with a feeling of contentment and excitement. The night had passed peacefully, and now she found herself smiling foolishly as she stretched luxuriously in the bed. This time tomorrow she would be Mrs. Alan d'Aprix. Of course, it wasn't a real marriage, and it wasn't going to last forever, but even so she was happy.

Her pleasurable musings were interrupted by a knock on the door, and she drew the covers around her as she sat up.

"Come in."

The door opened and Suzanne appeared, balancing a breakfast tray in one hand.

"Breakfast in bed?" she asked in surprise, disappointment tinging her voice. She had hoped to dine on the terrace with Alan, as had become their custom.

"Monsieur d'Aprix had to leave early to attend to some business," Suzanne explained apologetically. "But he said he will be back soon."

"I see. Well, then, I'll just enjoy this on my balcony. It looks delicious," she said brightly as she slipped into a robe and followed Suzanne outside.

"Take your time," Suzanne told her. "When you have eaten, I will be very happy to help you get ready for the ceremony."

They had agreed to have the ceremony at the house, on the terrace, with Suzanne and Jacques as witnesses. That was the most expedient procedure, considering the brief time they'd had to arrange things. She glanced at her watch and saw that it was time to get ready.

Her preparations didn't take long, although she was extra careful with her makeup and she brushed her hair more vigorously than usual until it lay in shining amber waves on her shoulders. Then she slipped the dress over her head, noting with satisfaction that it enhanced her natural femininity.

Just as she was tucking a last strand of hair into place

90

another knock sounded at the door. Assuming that it was Suzanne come back to offer assistance, Brooke called, "Come in," without turning from the mirror.

The door opened and Alan entered. He was impeccably dressed in a dove-gray suit that looked—and probably was—custom tailored. A silver and blue tie was at the neck of the pale blue shirt, and a boutonniere graced the lapel of the jacket. She drew her breath in sharply, an ache in her throat, as she gazed at his reflection in the mirror. If only she were really marrying him instead of entering into a business deal!

At that moment he caught sight of her, and she straightened and turned, her breath coming in shallow wisps.

For a long moment he didn't speak. His eyes moved slowly—almost hungrily, she thought—over her. She lowered her own eyes self-consciously under his lingering gaze. A flush of color stained her cheeks, and the gold tips of her lowered lashes were caught in the shaft of sunlight that streamed into the room.

When he still didn't speak, Brooke looked up expectantly, a light remark rising to her lips to ease the sudden tenseness in the room. But the words died in her throat when she saw his rigid mouth and narrowed eyes. She stared at him in astonishment, for the first time in their relationship feeling fear at the leashed emotion reflected in his face.

But when he caught her frightened gaze he forced the muscles in his face to relax. "You look lovely, Brooke. Just as a bride should." He smiled warmly, but his voice sounded strained. Then, as if suddenly remembering something, he glanced down at a box in his hands.

"These are for you. Every bride should have flowers." He handed her the box and she carefully opened it, not daring to look up and meet his eyes. If she did, he surely would see the love in them.

"Oh, Alan, they're beautiful!" she exclaimed as she

lifted out a corsage of miniature pink rosebuds and baby's breath.

"I'm glad you're pleased. Here, let me help you," he said as she fumbled with the pin. Deftly he pinned the flowers in place, and Brooke was conscious of his hands as they brushed her neck, and of his body so close to hers. She was filled with a longing so intense that she found herself trembling.

"Are you all right?" he asked in concern, his hands on her shoulders, his eyes anxiously searching her face.

She nodded mutely, unable to speak because of the lump in her throat. His tenderness only made it worse.

"You aren't regretting your decision, are you? It's not too late, you know. I don't want you to be sorry later, Brooke."

At last she found her voice.

"I'm fine, Alan. Just a case of pre-wedding jitters, I guess." Though she tried to hold her voice steady, a tremor ran through it. "Well," she took a deep breath and forced herself to smile up into his eyes, "I guess we're ready."

He slipped her arm through his and squeezed her hand. "I guess we are."

The ceremony was simple and brief, and Brooke felt almost like an observer. She heard someone answer, "I do," in the appropriate place, and to her surprise discovered that it was her own voice. Then a ring was being slipped on her finger and she heard the magistrate say, "I now pronounce you man and wife." She glanced up at Alan, but her view of his face was immediately blocked, for his lips came down on hers in a kiss as light as a drifting leaf that obliterated everything but the sound of drumming pulses.

The contact was all too brief, and then Alan was smiling down at her. She returned his smile automatically, unconsciously clinging to his arm, for her legs felt unsteady. In the eyes of the world she was now

Mrs. Alan d'Aprix, and though both she and Alan knew the true nature of their relationship, it was a heady feeling to actually be married to this man whom she had grown to love and respect. With a pang of bittersweet happiness, she resolved to enjoy every moment in the next couple of months. They would be all too fleeting, she was sure, but at least she'd have the memory of them to carry with her forever.

Alan had mentioned that he was a pilot, but Brooke was surprised when they flew to Paris in his private jet. By early evening they had settled into his fashionable Paris apartment for their "honeymoon." He preferred not to stay at his hotel when in Paris, he explained to her, saying that if he did he could never get away from business because he was too accessible.

They were greeted at the door upon their arrival by an older woman dressed in black, and while she watched with an indulgent smile Alan swept a surprised Brooke off her feet and carried her across the threshold.

"An American custom," he explained to the woman with a grin as he set Brooke on her feet. Before she could regain her composure, Alan was introducing her. "Brooke, this is Marie. She takes care of things for me here in Paris. Marie, this is my wife."

"It is a pleasure to meet you, madame," the woman said graciously. "I hope you will enjoy your stay in Paris. It is a beautiful city at any time, but especially when one is in love. I have prepared a special menu for your wedding night."

"I'm sure it will be wonderful," replied Alan as he put his arm around Brooke. Drawn into such intimate contact, his hand resting lightly on her hip, Brooke felt her composure melting. Her whole body was trembling slightly, and her concern increased when she began to wonder what arrangements had been made for the night. If this woman lived here, they couldn't very well go off to separate bedrooms on their wedding night!

A feeling of panic rose in her. What had she gotten herself into? Her eyes flew to Alan's face, but he was still speaking, and she forced herself to pay attention to what he was saying.

"Brooke and I are going to freshen up a bit while you finish making dinner, Marie." He picked up her overnight case, his arm still around her waist. "The luggage will be up in a few minutes," he said over his shoulder as he guided Brooke toward a door. She numbly allowed him to lead her, the full implication of her position suddenly overwhelming her. Only the click of the door closing behind them as they entered the bedroom broke her reverie.

With a start, she turned to stare at Alan, her eyes wide. Something of her panic communicated itself to him. He placed his hands on her shoulders and looked down at her. Under this close scrutiny she grew even more uncomfortable, and at last she dropped her eyes. He probably knew exactly what was going through her mind. What a naive fool he must think her! A sob rose in her throat. She would certainly be of no help to him in this condition.

"Brooke."

It was half question, half command. When she didn't respond, he spoke again, in a sterner tone.

"Brooke, look at me." His hands gripped her shoulders, and there was no denying the authority in that voice. She looked up and met his probing eyes squarely. For a moment he looked at her in silence, and when he spoke again his tone was tender.

"What's the matter? You aren't regretting your decision already, are you?"

"Oh, no," she assured him, her voice passionate. "I want to do everything I can to help you. It's just that..." Her voice trailed off, and she glanced unconsciously toward the bed. Noting the direction of her

94

glance, Alan's eyes twinkled mischievously.

"Ah, I think I see the light. But I thought we'd reached an understanding on that."

"I know," she replied. "But how will we manage? Won't it seem strange if we have separate bedrooms? I mean, when people are just married they usually..." She looked up at him for understanding, but he was regarding her with tolerant amusement. "I'm sorry, Alan," she whispered, a sob rising in her throat. "I know I'm being silly. It's just that I've never...this is the first time that..."

It was hopeless. How could she explain her feelings to him, a man of the world in every sense? She stood in miserable silence, and a tear ran silently down her cheek. Suddenly Alan pulled her close, his arms around her comfortingly.

"Brooke, I'm sorry," he apologized, his voice contrite. "I didn't mean to make light of your feelings. Of course this is all strange for you. I'm afraid I've been very insensitive. You don't have to worry about anything. As I told you before, this is strictly a business arrangement. That's all.

"And as far as the sleeping arrangements go," he gestured toward the bed, "you can have the master suite and I'll take the connecting guest room. It's rarely used, and Marie hardly ever goes in there. But I'll make the bed each morning, just in case. She only comes in during the day. And on the Riviera, you can have your old room. Suzanne and Jacques are the epitome of discretion. Does that make you feel any better?"

She nodded silently.

"Good." He placed his finger under her chin and tilted her face up so that their eyes met. "Now why don't you freshen up a bit before we have dinner." His finger traced the path of her tear. "After all, brides aren't supposed to cry. Marie will think I've been mistreating you.

"Until this deal is complete," he continued, 'we

have to play the part of newlyweds in public, but I hope we can still be friends in private. And there's no reason we can't have a good time. What do you say?"

Grateful for his understanding, Brooke nodded.

And they did, indeed, have a good time. The tension between them eased day by day into a comfortable familiarity, and for the next two weeks, when Alan wasn't attending to business, they toured Paris. The Eiffel Tower, the Louvre, Sacre Coeur, Notre Dame, even a trip to Versailles, were wonderful, but even more special to Brooke were the quiet moments they spent in quaint sidewalk cafes. To Brooke, Paris was the most beautiful city in the world, and she cherished each day she spent there with Alan.

Late one evening, as she brushed her hair in front of the dressing table in the guest bedroom—she had been adamant in her refusal to take Alan's room—she reflected back on their two weeks in the city. She had no idea how long he planned to stay in Paris, and although she knew he'd received many invitations to parties and dinners he'd refused them all, saying he was on his honeymoon and wanted to devote his time to his new wife. He had friends and acquaintances everywhere, though, and they rarely entered a theater or restaurant where he wasn't greeted by at least half-a-dozen people. On several occasions, flashbulbs had gone off in their faces. Society reporters, he'd told her.

Although he spent part of each day on business, he had not yet mentioned Nick Pappas, his Greek business associate. Since that was the reason for their "marriage," she thought this strange, but she was loathe to bring it up.

Besides, she was enjoying her role too much. Though he kept a discreet distance when they were alone, he had become accustomed to putting his arm around her waist and giving her endearing looks when they were in public, and she liked it.

She laid the brush on the dressing table and unclasped the thin gold chain that held a locket around her neck. She'd purchased it soon after their arrival in Paris, and now she carefully opened it. The pink rose petal inside had faded, but it still brought a smile to Brooke's lips. She knew she was being sentimental, but somehow she had wanted to preserve the memory of her wedding in a tangible way. A rose petal from her bouquet had been the most obvious choice, and she had worn it since then—inside her clothes, to avoid questions. Gently she laid it on the dressing table.

With a contented yawn she rose and carefully set her alarm clock. Marie came each day at nine, and Brooke made sure that the bed was made and her things removed before the woman arrived. As she placed the clock on the bedside table she caught a glimpse of herself in the full-length mirror on the opposite wall. She was wearing one of the satin and lace peignoir sets that Madame Barry had insisted upon— this one in shimmering pastel blue—and with a wry grin she let the robe slide off her shoulders to reveal the creamy expanse of her skin. Spaghetti straps and a deeply plunging neckline, which emphasized the gentle swell of her breasts, left much of the upper portion of her body bare. She gave the mirror a melancholy smile.

"Well, you're the only one who's ever going to see me in this," she told her reflection. "Wouldn't Madame Barry be disappointed?"

She climbed into bed and stared into the darkness. Each day her love for Alan grew, and the role of devoted wife was becoming easier to play all the time. Had she let her true feelings show? Did Alan suspect that she really loved him?

She fervently hoped not. She didn't want to make him feel guilty, for he'd done nothing to encourage her. She was sure that he thought of her only as an interesting and amusing companion rather than a desirable woman.

She heard Alan quietly preparing for bed in the adjacent room. It gave her a sense of security to know that he was near. Although he'd shown her the lock on the connecting door the first night, she had never felt the need to use it. Finally the soft noises in the next room ceased, and Brooke fell asleep.

She screamed. The headlights were coming closer. Never had the scene been so vivid. Suddenly someone grabbed her. She was being shaken. The headlights receded and in their place was blackness. Had she been hit by the car? She hadn't felt the impact.

"Are you all right, Brooke?"

Suddenly her eyes flew open and she realized she'd been dreaming. In the dim light coming through the door she recognized Alan sitting on the edge of her bed. His hands were on her shoulders in a grip so tight it was painful. She stared at him, her eyes wide. Then her face crumpled and her hands moved of their own volition to cover it. She was sitting bolt upright, her body rigid and clammy, and she shivered.

"It...it was the...nightmare again," she gasped, fighting to still the trembling of her body. "I've...had it...before...but never like this."

"It's O.K. now, Brooke. Just take some deep breaths." He gathered her in his arms as if she were a child, and she clung to him as she tried to steady the pounding of her heart. He didn't speak again, but his solid presence was reassurance enough that the nightmare was over. Gradually her body relaxed, and finally he held her at arm's length, his eyes searching her face.

"Better now?"

"Much." She noted that he was wearing only his pajama bottoms, and she realized that her screams must have catapulted him out of bed. The mental image that idea created suddenly seemed hilarious, and she began to giggle.

"What's wrong?" he demanded.

"N—nothing," she gasped. She felt rather giddy, and the harder she tried to control her laughter, the less success she had. Even Alan's dark frown didn't have its usual sobering effect. In an effort to control herself she looked down—and then her laughter died in her throat. While she'd been imagining his rapid response to her nightmare, she'd forgotten about her own scanty attire. Now, horrified, she realized that her nightgown was all too revealing, and in alarm she reached for the covers and drew them up. She looked up to find Alan watching her intently.

"I...I'm sorry. I guess it was just the relief," she whispered. "I'm fine now. Thank you for being here, Alan."

He didn't respond. Instead, he reached over and gently touched her cheek. Her breath caught in her throat, and she was unable to move. With his intense eyes boring into hers she felt herself being pulled toward him like a magnet.

He, too, seemed to be caught in a spell. They were inexorably drawn toward each other, and Brooke knew that she couldn't fight the force that had overtaken her. Alan put her hands on his shoulders, and with an almost savage ferocity pulled her toward him. She had only a quick glimpse of his fiercely burning eyes before his lips claimed hers.

Brooke had been kissed before, but never with such intensity. Her pulse beat frantically, and she clung to him, allowing his hands to mold her slim, pliant body to his. She responded to the pressure of his mouth with a passion she didn't know she possessed.

Her hands, which had automatically gone around his neck as he drew her toward him, now unconsciously pulled him even closer, and her lips hungrily moved over his as one of her hands buried itself in the soft hair at the back of his neck. With a groan he lowered her to the bed.

Although Brooke was barely conscious of her

actions—all she knew was that she was being swept along on a tide of overwhelmingly powerful emotion—somewhere in the back of her mind a warning bell sounded faintly. She tried to ignore it but, as Alan's hands began to move caressingly over her body, the uneasy warning became more insistent.

With a strength of will Brooke didn't think she possessed, she struggled to loosen the grip of his arms. For a moment he seemed oblivious to her attempts to break the embrace, but as she intensified her efforts he loosened his hold. Brooke pulled herself free and slid deftly off the bed. She stood staring down at him with wide eyes, one hand distractedly pushing her hair back from her face.

Had the situation not been so tense, Brooke would have found it laughable. Alan still lay on the bed, propped on one arm, a startled expression on his face. She couldn't blame him. She had run like a spooked deer, and he was probably not used to having his embraces rejected.

But she had done the right thing, she told herself staunchly. She would never have been able to live with herself if she'd succumbed to her desires. The silence lengthened uncomfortably, and Brooke searched for some way to break it.

"I'm sorry, Alan," she said shakily. "Things were getting out of hand, and this...wasn't part of our agreement."

By now he'd recovered sufficiently from his surprise to rise, and he stood looking down at her, his hands on his hips. His face was as strained and tense as her own, and when he spoke his voice, too, was shaken.

"I'm the one who should apologize," he said, letting his breath out slowly. "I had no right to do that."

Brooke swallowed the lump in her throat, interpreting the look in his eyes for anger. She shivered and his eyes narrowed.

"You'd better get back into bed. You'll catch cold if you stand there like that." He walked toward the bedroom door, pausing at the threshold to turn and look at her. "You needn't worry, Brooke. I won't bother you again," he said with deadly finality.

The door clicked shut behind him, and silent tears ran down Brooke's cheeks.

## Chapter Nine

The easy companionship between them was now gone, Brooke discovered the next morning. By the time she got up, after a nearly sleepless night of tossing and turning, Alan had already left. A cryptic note lay on the kitchen counter.

Brooke—
Business to attend to all day. Won't be back till late. Don't wait up. Should conclude all Paris business tomorrow and we can leave for the Riviera day after.

Alan

The cold, impersonal note had an unmistakably businesslike tone. But, after all, she realized with a start, that was all they really were—business associates. Brooke had made it clear in no uncertain terms last night that she wanted—and intended—to keep their relationship on that level, and Alan was responding accordingly. She couldn't blame him. Men like Alan probably weren't used to rejection.

But it was best this way, she told herself resolutely. Besides, in the light of day he was probably glad for what had happened. She knew he didn't love her, didn't want any commitments, and this way he didn't have to feel any obligation to her. When the business deal was concluded he could watch her leave with a clear conscience. In the long run he would realize that she had actually done him a favor.

True to his word, Alan didn't come back to the apartment during the day. Brooke tried to amuse herself with reading, but she couldn't concentrate. Her thoughts kept turning to Alan and their encounter the previous evening, and though he wasn't physically near her, the memory of his arms about her set her pulses drumming.

Finally, unable to endure the gloomy quiet of the apartment any longer, she rose and picked up the tweed jacket which matched her gray slacks.

"Marie, I'm going out for a walk," she said.

The housekeeper looked up from her dusting.

"Oui, madame. Is there anything you would like me to do while you are gone?"

"No, thanks. M. d'Aprix probably won't be home until late, so when you're finished feel free to leave. I may not be back for quite some time."

"Oui, madame."

For a while Brooke strolled aimlessly around the fashionable residential district in which Alan's apartment was located. The late afternoon air was crisp, hinting at the change of season to come. With a determined effort she tried to shake off her deepening gray mood, forcing herself to take note of her surroundings. A sidewalk cafe on the next corner looked inviting, and she decided to stop for something to drink.

Absently her long, slender fingers with their subtly polished nails toyed with the glass of lemonade in front of her. Chin in hand, she forced herself to examine the situation as objectively as she could.

Fact: Alan d'Aprix had hit her with his car and subsequently taken care of her until she was back on her feet again.

Fact: He had asked her to become his wife for a short time until he concluded an important business deal.

Fact: Sometime between the moment his car struck her and the moment he asked her to marry him she had fallen in love with him.

Fact: He was not in love with her and never would be.

Fact: Being in his presence day after day, posing as his adoring bride, was playing havoc with her nerves.

Having reduced the situation to stark simplicity, Brooke arrived at two questions: first, could she maintain her poise without giving away her true feelings, and second, even if she could carry that off, would she be devastated emotionally in doing so?

Unconsciously her fingers gently touched her lips and she closed her eyes. She could still feel the hard, demanding pressure of Alan's mouth as his lips had claimed hers last night. Looking back on the scene now, she didn't know how she had had the strength of will to put a stop to it when she did.

With a sigh, she settled her bill and then rose and slowly made her way back to the apartment. She supposed she'd have to go through with the agreement. She wasn't a quitter, and Alan was counting on her. But it was becoming harder and harder to switch back and forth between playing a devoted wife in public and being strictly a friend and business associate in private.

Marie was gone by the time Brooke returned to the apartment, but she'd left a note saying that dinner was in the oven. Without much interest Brooke opened the door and peered inside, carefully lifting the cover on the plate. Even an appetizing array of fresh vegetables and a chicken breast covered with a rich sauce couldn't tempt Brooke's appetite, but she set a place for herself and listlessly picked at her food. Where was Alan eating dinner? Was he still angry at her about last night? When would he be home?

By the time Brooke had prepared for bed and crawled under the covers it was after eleven. Alan still had not arrived, and though she tried to sleep she found herself listening for the sound of his key in the lock.

It was a long wait. The hands of the clock pointed to two thirty before she finally heard him moving about in the next room. She wondered dejectedly if he had sought comfort and love from a more willing partner before coming home.

Finally the muffled sounds from the adjacent room ceased, but it wasn't until much later that she fell into a troubled sleep.

Brooke had hoped to be awake by the time Alan left the next morning, but it was eight thirty before she awoke. Apparently she'd forgotten to set the alarm clock. Hastily she threw on her clothes and made up the bed, for Marie would be at the apartment promptly at nine. She had barely finished applying her makeup and depositing her nightgown in a dresser drawer, when she heard the woman letting herself in the front door.

"Good morning, Marie," she called a bit breathlessly, emerging from Alan's room.

"Good morning, madame. I will be most happy to fix you some breakfast if you are just rising."

"Thanks, but I'm just going to have some juice," she called over her shoulder as she headed for the kitchen. She wanted to get there first in case Alan had left a note.

Quickly her eyes scanned the counter and came to rest on a folded sheet of paper. With a quick movement she was across the room, and rapidly her eyes read the few hastily scribbled words.

Brooke:
   I'll be finishing my business by late afternoon.

Let's plan to leave Paris tonight.

Alan

That was it. Brooke stared in dismay at the note. Was he still angry at her? Why was he so obviously avoiding her? Was he sorry now that he'd asked her to play the part of his wife? Had she become a liability, a complication, instead of an asset?

Brooke spent the day preparing to leave, noting that Alan's bags were already packed and waiting by the door. By the time four o'clock came, and with it Alan's imminent arrival, her nerves were at the snapping point. She had dressed with extra care, donning a pale green sheath that was cinched tightly at the waist with a wide leather belt. She had also taken unusual pains with her hair and makeup. Now she sat waiting in the living room, anxiously twisting her hands in her lap.

"If there is nothing else, madame, I will be going."

Marie's voice startled Brooke and she jumped.

"Oh! No, no there's nothing else. We'll be leaving tonight, you know. I'm sure M. d'Aprix will leave instructions for you."

"Merci, madame. I hope your stay in Paris has been most happy. But when we are in love, it matters not where we are, n'est-ce pas? And I can tell that you are very much in love."

Brooke turned shocked eyes on the woman, nervously twisting the thin gold chain around her neck. Either she had been an excellent actress or the woman had discerned her true feelings. She sincerely hoped it was the former.

"Paris is a wonderful city," Brooke replied noncommittally.

"You will see much more of it in the future, I am sure. Well, until your next visit, au revoir."

*There won't be a next visit*, Brooke said silently as the door closed behind Marie. Restlessly she rose and began pacing as she waited for Alan. Finally tiring, she sat again, only to jump up a moment later when the door opened. In agitation she turned to face the man across from her.

At first he seemed taken aback by her appearance—*it's almost as if he's forgotten I exist*, Brooke thought with a pang—and then he recovered and casually strolled toward her, pausing to drop his briefcase in a chair. For a moment he looked at her through enigmatic eyes, his face devoid of all expression.

"Well, Brooke, it seems we've run into a bit of difficulty." His cool tone suggested that he was addressing a stranger, and his manner was so impersonal that she found it hard to believe he was the man with whom she had laughingly explored the Eiffel Tower and eaten French pastry at a sidewalk cafe on the Champs Elysees. "First, let me apologize again for the other night. I made a promise to you, and I broke it. No excuses. If you want to call off our arrangement now, I'll understand perfectly."

Brooke stared at him. Was he sincerely offering her a way out, if she felt unable to continue? Or was he suggesting in a subtle way that he had had enough and wanted her to leave?

"Well, I made a promise, too," she replied hesitantly.

"Then you're willing to continue?"

His voice was so icy she shivered. He didn't seem to care one way or the other what she decided. But she'd never backed out on a deal in her life, and she wasn't going to begin now.

"I—I guess so."

"I need a firmer commitment than that, Brooke, if we're going to carry this off," he said impatiently. "Things will become much more demanding when we get back to the coast. If you don't think you can handle it, now is the time to get out."

"I can handle it!" she snapped indignantly. He was making it sound like this whole thing was her fault!

Well, if he could be so cool, so could she! Two could play that game.

"Fine." He picked up his briefcase and glanced at his watch. "Can you be ready in half an hour? I'll have the bags taken to the plane and we can be in the air in a couple of hours."

"I'm ready now."

"Good. I'm going to grab a sandwich first. Have you eaten?"

His question was almost an afterthought, and though her heart was aching at his impersonal attitude, she forced herself to adopt an equally cool tone.

"I'm not hungry."

"Suit yourself," he shrugged. "But it will be hours before we arrive."

"I said I'm not hungry."

Three hours later, sitting next to Alan in the cockpit of the plane, she was sorry she hadn't taken his advice. Her stomach was rumbling noisily, and she glanced at him surreptitiously, wondering if he'd heard the betraying sound. Without a word he reached behind him, one hand still on the wheel, and withdrew a paper bag.

"I packed a couple of extra sandwiches in case I got hungry on the trip. Help yourself if you want something," he remarked, depositing the sack between them.

Brooke eyed it hungrily, but she kept her arms crossed.

"Hand me an apple, would you?" he asked.

Silently she dug into the bag, withdrew a glossy piece of fruit, and handed it to him.

"There's another one in there if you'd like it."

With a sigh Brooke gave in to her growing hunger pangs and pulled out the other apple, munching in silence. Alan finished first, and when he'd deposited the core in a trash container he spoke.

"Let me brief you on what's been happening so

109

you'll be prepared when we land in Nice," he said in a businesslike tone. "Nick Pappas called while we were in Paris to congratulate me on my marriage, and he insisted on meeting you. So I've arranged a reception at the Riviera house for the day after tomorrow. Suzanne is taking care of all the details, so you won't have to worry about anything. Nick will be there, of course, and so will a number of my friends and business associates. That will be the first big test of your skills as an actress. I realize it may be difficult in light of what's happened, but you'll have to act the part of a happy bride, no matter how repugnant that may be to you."

Brooke bit her lip to stop herself from correcting him. It was apparent Alan had taken her rebuff of his advances as an indication that she was not attracted to him. Perhaps it was best if he believed that. It would probably prevent any recurrence of such emotionally charged scenes. Few men had egos strong enough to risk rejection by the same woman twice.

"Do you think you're up to a party like that?" he interrupted her thoughts.

"I'm sure I can handle it," she said with more confidence than she felt.

"Good." He gave a satisfied nod and lapsed into silence. It was obvious that his mind was elsewhere, and Brooke made no attempt to break into his thoughts. She was occupied with too many of her own.

First on the agenda after they landed was a trip to see Dr. Lafitte, who pronounced her much improved, despite the extra walking in Paris.

"You may need to favor the knee a bit now and then if you are on your feet for long stretches, but you should not have any real problems," he told her. "Besides," he added with a wink, "you can always lean on your new husband."

Brooke looked at Alan uncomfortably and adjusted a button on her blouse so she wouldn't have to meet the doctor's eyes, but Alan smiled at the remark and then solicitously placed an arm around her waist as they left the office. Despite his coolness when they were alone, she still found herself trembling when his arm was around her.

While he attended to business that afternoon, Brooke consulted with Suzanne on plans for the reception. When it became apparent that Suzanne had things well in hand, Brooke retreated to the living room to write Mary. She had dropped her a short note shortly after the accident, explaining where she was and that she would be delayed returning, promising to write again as soon as she had a chance.

Brooke spent a long time composing the letter, for it was difficult to talk about her marriage without revealing its true nature, and she couldn't do that yet, not even to Mary. So she skirted the issue, talking instead about Alan's beautiful home on the Riviera and their stay in Paris.

Alan had told Brooke that he would again be working late, so she ate a solitary dinner on the terrace and went to bed early.

The next day passed quickly. Brooke insisted upon helping Suzanne with the party preparations. It kept her mind off the fact that Alan had become almost invisible, studiously avoiding any contact with her. When they were together at meals an awkward stiffness existed between them. He was polite, but cool. He didn't seem angry. In fact, that was just the problem. He showed no emotion. For him, it seemed, their relationship was—and had always been—just a matter of business, and only in a moment of emotional weakness had he allowed for the possibility of anything more.

Brooke dressed carefully for the evening, realizing that the impression she made tonight on Alan's friends and business associates was very important. She had chosen a backless, halter-style dress with a low scoop neckline. It was made of layers of lightweight sapphire blue material, shot through with silver threads. The bodice hugged her tightly, and the full skirt was a swirling cloud that billowed as she walked. Finally she strapped on low-heeled silver sandals.

Next she applied her makeup carefully and took pains to highlight her eyes with mascara and a faint silvery blue shadow. She brushed her hair vigorously until it shone, and then on one side pinned a silver-blue flower of the same material as her dress.

She stepped back from the full-length mirror and surveyed her reflection. The dress was far more dramatic and sophisticated than any she had yet worn, but it showed off her figure to perfection. *Was it too daring?* she wondered, a worried frown on her face. Madame Barry had assured her that it would be perfectly appropriate for her new life, and she had taken the woman's word. But now she was torn by doubts.

A knock sounded on the door, and in a distracted voice she called, "Come in." She heard the door open, but when there was no further sound from the person who had entered she turned curiously.

Alan, dressed in a black tuxedo complete with bow tie and ruffled shirt, was standing on the threshold, and Brooke felt her senses stirring at the sight of his masculine form, which was enhanced by the formal dress. He looked at her without speaking, his eyes taking in every detail of her appearance, and at last she turned back toward the mirror in confusion. Maybe he didn't like the dress.

"Is it too much? I...I don't have much experience with these types of parties. Madame Barry said it would be fine for such occasions, but..." Her voice trailed off uncertainly, her doubts resurfacing. She turned back to him, her anxiety reflected in her eyes.

"It's quite lovely, Brooke," he assured her, his voice tinged with warmth. "I'm sure you'll charm all the guests." He entered the room and walked toward her. Unconsciously she took a step backward, and she saw his eyes narrow at her action. He stopped his advance immediately, and after a moment he reached into his pocket and withdrew an oblong case.

"It's only appropriate that a bride have jewels," he said as he handed it to her.

Silently she took it and lifted the lid, her eyes riveted to his. When she glanced down a gasp escaped from her lips. A silver, diamond-encrusted necklace lay on a velvet bed. She stared at it in awe for a few moments and then looked up.

"I can't accept this, Alan," she whispered.

"You don't like it?"

"It's beautiful! But you've given me far too much already."

"The necklace will enhance that lovely dress. And my guests will expect my bride to have jewels."

She looked down at the exquisite necklace in her hands. It was so tempting....

"Well, maybe I could wear it—just for tonight."

"Let me help you." Before she could protest he took the necklace from her hands and, with deft fingers that were cool against her neck, fastened the clasp. Then he stood back and examined her critically. "Just right. Shall we go and meet our guests?" He offered her his arm and she took it mutely, all too aware of the warmth of his body so close to hers. With a deep breath she steeled herself for the ordeal to come.

## Chapter Ten

The drawing room was already filled with people when they entered. A hush fell over the group as she and Alan stood together in the doorway, and at the faint but insistent pressure on her arm she looked up at him. He smiled, and his eyes encouraged her to smile, too.

Gently he drew her toward the first cluster of people, and as they moved from group to group she found herself smiling and nodding and making what she hoped were appropriate and intelligent comments.

Sometime during their circuit of the room Alan's arm had slipped to her waist, and his hand rested lightly on her hip. She was intensely aware of their physical nearness, and without even being conscious of her actions she moved closer to him. He was playing the part of the amiable host and happy bridegroom so well that she was almost fooled herself. He laughed and chatted and deferred to her on several questions, and soon she found herself relaxing and actually enjoying the party. As they moved away from one group he leaned down and whispered to her.

"You're doing fine, Brooke. Our most important guest has just arrived." He nodded toward the door and Brooke looked in that direction. A middle-aged man, short and balding, was just entering the room. "I know Nick's anxious to meet you, so let's not keep him waiting." He tightened his grip, gave her an encouraging squeeze, and led her toward the rather rotund man.

"Ah, Alan. I have awaited this moment with pleasure."

"Nick, I'd like you to meet my wife, Brooke. Brooke, Nick Pappas."

"How do you do, Nick. Alan has told me so much about you."

"All good, I hope," he replied in accented speech, his eyes twinkling. "You know, when I read that Alan had finally gotten married I could not believe it. He has been such a confirmed bachelor," the older man wagged his finger teasingly at Alan. "But now that I see you in person I can understand why he was swept away by your charms. Your pictures do not do you justice."

"Pictures?"

"But of course! In all the society columns. You mean that you have not seen them? Ah, Alan, you are indeed fortunate. You have not married a vain woman. I hope you realize how lucky you are."

"Indeed I do," Alan replied, and when he smiled down at Brooke she could almost believe he meant it.

They chatted for a few minutes, and then Nick excused himself. "I see someone over there I must speak with," he apologized. "But I will talk with you both later."

"You were a hit, Brooke," Alan commented when the older man was out of earshot.

"Do you think so?" she asked anxiously. "I know how important this deal is to you. Funny, he didn't even seem upset about our marriage. I thought he would be outraged on behalf of his daughter. From what you said I thought he practically had you both to the altar."

"I suppose he's had time to adjust to the fact. Nick is

116

a realist above all else." Alan shrugged, dismissing the subject. Then he switched the topic. "How is your knee holding out?"

"Pretty well. But it would be nice to sit down for a few minutes," she admitted.

Alan looked around and spotted an empty chair off to one side of the room.

"I have just the spot," he said as he led her to it. "You rest here a minute and I'll go and get something for us to eat."

From this vantage point, half hidden by a full-leafed Kentia palm, Brooke was able to study the guests in the room. She had seen gatherings like this before—men in tuxedos, women in evening gowns and dripping with jewels—but only in movies. That she was part of such a glittering scene was almost beyond her comprehension.

Suddenly a movement in the doorway caught her attention. Standing on the threshold, in an almost theatrical pose, was a striking dark-haired woman in a strapless red dress. It clung to her body and was deeply slit on one side, emphasizing her dramatically stunning good looks.

Brooke found herself staring at this latest arrival. Others in the room were also looking at the woman—although in a more discreet manner than Brooke—and a low rumble of talk replaced the laughter and sometimes shrill voices of the women that had filled the room a moment before.

Curiously Brooke looked around for Alan. She saw him, his back to the door, talking intently with Nick. Apparently he was unaware of the woman's entrance. Brooke looked back toward the door. The woman's eyes were searching the room, but suddenly they stopped, and a satisfied smile appeared on her face. With a lithe movement she made her way toward Alan and tapped him on the shoulder.

Frowning slightly at the interruption, he turned, and

117

immediately the woman threw her arms around him and kissed him directly on the mouth. Brooke's own mouth dropped open in surprise. Alan, too, seemed somewhat taken aback, but a moment later he firmly but gently disentangled himself from the woman's embrace. Even then she kept one arm linked in his.

"Alan, you naughty boy! Getting married without even inviting me to the wedding! How could you?" The woman's voice was pitched slightly above those of the other guests, and it carried clearly to Brooke.

"Hello, Monique. What a surprise. I thought you were in Italy on holiday." Alan had quickly recovered his composure, and he spoke in controlled, well-modulated tones.

"I was, darling. But then I heard about your marriage, and I came back just as quickly as I could. I wanted to congratulate you and meet your bride."

Brooke rose, and the movement caught Monique's eye. Her face grew hard and her eyes narrowed when she saw the young woman in blue and silver, and Brooke realized the woman must be one of Alan's old flames.

"Here she is now," Alan replied, and Brooke thought she detected a note of relief in his voice. He removed himself from Monique's clasp and went to meet Brooke, drawing her close to him as they turned to face the woman. "Brooke, I'd like you to meet Monique Chere, a long-time acquaintance of mine. Monique, this is my wife, Brooke."

The woman smiled at Brooke, a smile that didn't quite reach her eyes. "A pleasure," she said with saccharine sweetness, her eyes on Brooke's necklace.

"Thank you," replied Brooke. "It's nice to meet so many of Alan's friends."

"Well, as one of Alan's dearest...friends," Monique paused at the word and gave him a significant look, "let me be one of the first to congratulate you. We must get together for lunch sometime."

118

Brooke was surprised at the offer, but she recovered quickly and smiled. "That would be nice."

"Good. Well, Alan, I must circulate." In a waft of perfume she was gone.

"Monique can be a bit overpowering when you first meet her," Alan remarked, his eyes on the retreating figure. Then he turned toward Brooke. "I was interrupted on my way to the buffet. Shall we go and see what Suzanne has prepared?"

Brooke nodded and allowed him to lead her to the table. Apparently he was not going to comment any further on Monique, and Brooke didn't have time to ask any questions because they were intercepted by Nick.

"Alan, I must be going. But I wanted to suggest that you and your lovely wife join me on my yacht in Greece next week. It would be a nice vacation for you and Brooke—sort of an extended honeymoon," he smiled. "And it would give us a chance to discuss the land business further. I would like to finish that up as soon as possible."

"That would be fine, Nick," Alan replied. Brooke excused herself while they worked out the details.

A few minutes later Alan joined her at the buffet table. Then they once again moved from group to group, chatting with the guests. Slowly the people began leaving, and, though sorry to see the party end, Brooke was glad that she would soon be able to sit down.

"Now don't forget, we must have lunch soon," Monique reminded Brooke at the door. "I understand you're going to Greece, so I'll ring you when you return."

Brooke was a bit taken aback at how fast news traveled.

As the door closed behind the last guest, she wearily rubbed her neck. Her fingers met the clasp of her necklace and, with a quick movement, she unsnapped it and handed the piece of jewelry to Alan.

"I'll feel much better if you take care of this," she said.

He took it without comment and dropped it casually into the pocket of his jacket. "Tired?"

"Mmmm," she nodded.

"It was a long evening," he admitted. "But it was necessary. My friends and business associates would have been insulted if I hadn't invited them to meet you."

"I didn't mind," Brooke assured him. "I felt like a princess in this dress, with that necklace..." The words "and with a handsome man like you" sprang to her lips, but she caught herself in time.

He seemed about to make some comment on that remark, but instead he turned abruptly away.

"You'd better get some rest," he said over his shoulder as he walked toward his private suite. "We'll be leaving for Greece in a few days, and I'm sure you'll enjoy it more if you're well rested. Good night."

Brooke stared after him as the door closed. So much for her fairy-tale evening. Now that the guests were gone, Alan had made it clear that there was no need to keep up the act. With drooping shoulders she turned and walked slowly toward her room.


Despite the strained atmosphere between them, Brooke found herself looking forward to the trip to Greece. She'd never been on a yacht, and she had liked Nick immediately. It would be a good chance to soak up some sun and enjoy what remained of her life of luxury.

Several days later, as she stepped out of a limousine at the dock in Piraeus, Brooke gazed about her in delight. Yachts of every size and description were in the harbor, and before she could ask the question that came immediately to mind, Alan pointed out one of the larger ones.

"That's Nick's. He doesn't believe in doing anything on a small scale, as you can see."

"I believe it!" she exclaimed.

Alan took her elbow and led her toward the vessel. It was called "The Daphne," Brooke noted, after Nick's daughter. Would she be on board? What would her attitude be? Brooke didn't look forward to meeting her, even though Alan had assured her several times that he had never had any serious intentions toward the woman.

Nick greeted them cordially as they came aboard and ushered them onto the deck.

"Would you like something to drink?" he asked.

"Brooke?" Alan inquired.

"Just a fruit punch, please."

"A wise woman," Nick nodded approvingly. "I wish my daughter would adopt the same practice."

"Is Daphne aboard?" Alan asked casually.

"Not yet. But she will join us before we sail tonight. Alan, what will you have?"

While he gave the white-coated steward their orders, Brooke glanced around the yacht, her eyes sparkling. It was like a movie set. Everything was shining as if it were constantly being scrubbed and polished, and the gleaming copper provided a nice contrast to the deep blue of the sea.

"I see you approve of my little ship," Nick remarked to her with a smile.

"It's beautiful!" she exclaimed. "Thank you so much for inviting us aboard."

"You are very welcome, my dear. You must allow me to give you a tour later."

"I'd enjoy that."

"Well now," he took a sip of his drink and rose, "I will give you a little while to settle into your cabin." He motioned to a crewman over his shoulder, and instantly the man was beside him. "Victor will show you the way. Shall we meet for dinner about eight?"

121

"That sounds fine." Alan rose, taking Brooke's hand and drawing her up beside him.

They followed Victor below deck and down a long, narrow corridor lined with doors. Finally he stopped and opened one, stepping aside to allow Brooke and Alan to enter.

"Your luggage has been put into the bedroom," Victor said. "If there is anything else you need, just press the button." He indicated a small disc unobtrusively located next to the door. "Is there anything I can do for you now?"

"No thanks. Everything is fine," Alan told him.

"Very well," Victor replied, walking toward the door. "Enjoy your stay."

As the door shut behind him Brooke eagerly looked over the cabin. The sitting room was tastefully furnished in subtle shades of gray and wine, and a vase of fresh flowers stood on the table along with a basket of fruit. A curtained archway led to the bedroom, which continued the color scheme of the sitting room. Brooke was about to exclaim over the elegance of the cabin when it suddenly occurred to her that there was only one bedroom. She turned to Alan in alarm.

He had been watching her reactions to the graciousness of the suite with amused tolerance, but now he frowned.

"What's wrong?"

"There's only one bedroom," she blurted out.

"Naturally," he said with scorn. "If you were Nick, wouldn't you assume that newlyweds would want to sleep together?"

The bluntness—and truth—of his statement made her blush, and she looked down. "I suppose so," she admitted.

"You needn't worry," he assured her harshly. "I'll sleep out here on the couch. It will only be for a few days."

Brooke eyed the small settee doubtfully. There was

no way that Alan would be able to get a comfortable night's sleep on it. He was much too tall.

"Let me sleep out here," she suggested. "I'm a lot smaller than you are and I'll fit much—"

"I'm sleeping here," he interrupted her. The curtness and finality of his tone discouraged argument, and Brooke shrugged.

"Suit yourself," she replied, using anger to mask the hurt inflicted by his indifference.

They took turns in the well-appointed bath, and didn't speak again until it was time to go back upstairs for dinner. Brooke discreetly closed the curtains across the archway while she dressed, vitally aware of Alan's presence on the other side of the flimsy drape. Although he was cooly courteous to her when they were alone, he carefully avoided any physical contact and kept conversation to a minimum. But his public manner, warm and solicitous, and his habit of putting his arm intimately around her waist, still caused her heart to pound. It gave her a glimpse of what life with Alan could be like if he loved her. She wasn't sure how much longer she could bear living like this.

She put the final touches on her hair and stood back to examine herself in the mirror. The deep gold of her dress gave a warm glow to her complexion, and the cowl neckline of the chiffon fell in soft folds. The skirt draped gracefully around her hips and hung in filmy folds. She'd added gold sandals and a simple gold pendant, and the effect was feminine and youthful. Satisfied, she turned away and walked toward the drape.

"May I come in?" she called hesitantly.

"Yes."

Alan was adjusting his tie in the mirror, and once again she admired his lean good looks. Tonight he wore a white dinner jacket and black slacks. She stood quietly until he finished, and when he turned his eyes swept over her. It was a brief but thorough scrutiny, and she waited for his comment. But none came, and disappointment welled up in her. With an effort she kept her face immobile. He glanced at his watch and moved toward the door.

"We'll have to hurry or we'll be late. Nick doesn't like to be kept waiting."

Wordlessly she joined him at the door, and she noticed that he was careful to move aside so she wouldn't brush him as she passed. Had he come to hate her that much? A sick feeling came over her at the thought. She had always known that she could never win his love, but she had at least harbored the hope they could remain friends. Now that hope seemed shattered.

As they prepared to emerge on deck, Alan took her arm. She stiffened at his touch, and he whispered close to her ear.

"You'll have to do better than that, Brooke. I know you'd rather not have me touch you, but it can't be helped. Nick is a shrewd man. He'll see right through this masquerade if you don't loosen up."

Brooke forced her muscles to relax and her lips to curve into the semblance of a smile.

Nick and a young woman were already on deck when Alan and Brooke arrived, and they turned in greeting as the couple approached them. Brooke eyed the woman with trepidation. She was taller than Brooke by at least three inches and was rather athletic in build, though shapely as well. She was dressed in a simple frock of deep rose that complemented her dark hair and tanned complexion. She wore little makeup on her open, friendly face, and Brooke found her fear evaporating.

"Brooke, how lovely you look this evening," Nick greeted her cordially. "I would like to present my daughter, Daphne. Daphne, this is Alan's wife, Brooke."

"Hello, Brooke. And congratulations. How you managed to catch one of the most eligible bachelors in

Europe is beyond me. Heavens knows, others have tried." She turned to Alan. "So, Alan, you finally did it. Haven't I been telling you for years that you needed a wife?"

Brooke looked at the woman curiously, searching for some sign of disappointment or animosity. But there was none. *What an incredibly graceful loser*, she thought admiringly. Whenever she thought about losing Alan—well, that wasn't quite correct. She couldn't lose something she never had. But if Daphne was crushed, she was hiding it well.

"Daphne almost did not make the trip," Nick was grumbling good-naturedly. "She was playing in one of her everlasting tennis tournaments."

"How did you do?" Alan asked her.

"She won," Nick answered proudly.

"Oh, Papa," Daphne protested. "It was only a small tournament."

"Congratulations," Alan smiled warmly, and then turned to Brooke. "I've faced this woman on a court before, and let me tell you, she is a demon when she gets a racket in her hand."

"Do you play tennis, Brooke?" Daphne asked.

"I'm afraid not," Brooke admitted. "I've never really had the chance to learn. But I admire anyone who is good in sports," she added sincerely.

They continued to chat amiably, and throughout dinner the conversation flowed freely. Brooke kept searching for some sign of anger or jealousy in the woman across from her, but found none. Daphne seemed in good spirits and chatted animatedly during the meal. Brooke soon began to relax and enjoy herself. The confrontation she had most dreaded was over, and it had passed smoothly and without tension.

Brooke commented on that to Alan when they returned to their cabin later in the evening, but he just shrugged it off.

"Daphne is quite adept at hiding her feelings. Besides, I think it was more of a passing crush than anything. Once she realized that I was married she probably turned her attention elsewhere."

Alan's casual tone was not altogether convincing. Had he been completely honest about his reasons for this "business relationship" marriage? Brooke's sudden doubts surprised her. But it didn't matter. The charade would soon be over, and for the next few days she could relax and soak up some sun.

Daphne and Brooke spent a considerable amount of time together while Alan and Nick discussed business, and her hostess's manner continued to be open and friendly. Brooke was tempted to ask some discreet questions about her relationship with Alan, but she couldn't think of a good way to broach the subject. If the other woman was truly hurt and struggling to hide her feelings, it would be cruel to touch on the subject. Finally, Brooke gave up on the idea.

On their last day at sea, they were lying in the sun on deck chairs, talking of inconsequential things, when Daphne remarked that she'd played in a tennis tournament recently in Paris.

"Oh, I was just there," Brooke said. "It's a lovely city."

"I know," Daphne agreed. "Alan has a hotel there, I believe. You were there on your honeymoon, weren't you?"

"Yes," Brooke replied, glad that her floppy hat and sunglasses hid most of her face.

"It's a wonderful place for people in love. There's something magic about Paris. I bet you enjoyed your stay."

Brooke smiled as she remembered their first days in the city. It had been so wonderful to see the sights with Alan.

"I can see you did." Daphne was looking at her with a smile. "You're very much in love, aren't you? It shows in your eyes. I'm glad. Alan deserves to be loved

126

truly—for himself—not for his position or wealth. He was lucky to find you, and I think he realizes that. It's beautiful to watch two people so much in love. It's not something you see very often anymore."

Brooke didn't comment. Apparently her love was obvious—at least to everyone except Alan. For that Brooke was grateful. No acting had been required on her part. But apparently Alan had done an admirable job with his own acting if he had fooled Daphne.

They had a gala farewell dinner that evening, with Nick toasting the newlyweds and the business arrangement that Alan and he had finalized. Alan had not mentioned the land deal to Brooke since they'd arrived, but apparently, from the gay atmosphere at dinner, things had gone well.

With a pang Brooke realized that soon Alan's need for her would end. During dinner she forced herself to laugh in all the right places and to make the right responses to questions, but her heart was breaking. She picked at her food, and she was glad when the evening was finally over and they could return to their cabin.

"You didn't seem yourself tonight, Brooke," Alan commented when they were alone. "Aren't you feeling well?"

"I'm fine," she replied noncommittally. Then, though she dreaded to hear the answer, she forced herself to ask, "Did things work out well in your business with Nick?"

"Yes. We've agreed in principle to all of the points. Now we just have to have the papers drawn up and signed. That will probably take another couple of weeks."

He made no mention of her departure, and Brooke didn't bring the subject up. It would have to be discussed soon enough. In the meantime, maybe she could recapture some of their easy camaraderie. She didn't want to leave on such a sour note.

Surely Alan couldn't hate her just because of that

one incident. He must realize by now that in many ways she was old-fashioned—at least when it came to sexual morality—however archaic that sounded. She knew he could never love her, but she longed for their former friendly relationship. She had a couple of weeks left to work on it, according to Alan's estimate of when the deal would be completed. Maybe by the time she left they could once more be on friendly terms.

With that positive thought she fell asleep.

# Chapter Eleven

Despite Brooke's optimistic plan, she quickly discovered on their return journey that its chances for success were minimal. Although she tried to keep up a running stream of chatty banter, Alan responded as briefly as possible. His thoughts seemed thousands of miles away.

His jaw was set in a hard line and his eyes stared ahead moodily out the cockpit window. His long, slender fingers rested on the wheel, and one of them tapped the rim impatiently. He had probably forgotten all about her, she thought gloomily, now that her usefulness was almost finished. At last she gave up the struggle to draw him into conversation and lapsed into silence.

They spoke hardly a word during the rest of the flight and during the drive to his home. With a curt, "Let's have dinner at eight," he left her standing in the drawing room while he closed the door to his study.

His dismal mood had not improved by dinner, and Brooke practically choked on her food when she tried to swallow. They parted with only a few words to each other, and Brooke spent a sleepless night. In the early hours of the morning she rose and restlessly walked over to the window, noting with surprise that the light in Alan's study was still on. *Probably working on an-*

*other business deal*, she thought bitterly.

During the next few days Alan established a pattern of leaving early and returning late, so Brooke rarely saw him. She spent her days by the pool reading, walking around the garden, or helping Jacques care for the flowers. If he and his wife thought her and Alan's behavior strange, they made no comment, and Brooke was grateful for their discretion.

One day when Brooke returned to the house after a brief walk she found a strange car in the driveway. Eagerly she quickened her pace, for any company was better than the solitude to which she had been confined since her return from Greece.

To her surprise, no one was in the living room when she entered, and she walked toward the terrace thinking that perhaps the visitor was waiting there. She was only halfway across the room when a movement almost out of her line of vision caught her eye, and she turned.

Monique, in an apricot-colored suit with designer lines, was entering the room from the hall. Brooke stared at her. What had the woman been doing in that wing of the house? There were only bedrooms there—including hers—Brooke realized with a sudden surge of panic. She'd left her door open this morning, and her things were in plain view on the dressing table and in the wardrobe, so if Monique had ventured that far she must have seen them.

For her part, Monique seemed equally taken aback at the sight of Brooke, but she recovered quickly and smiled—a smug smile that told Brooke the woman had indeed seen her room.

"Oh, there you are, Brooke," she said sweetly. "Suzanne let me in and while I waited I thought I'd take a look around. Alan has had some redecorating done recently and I wanted to see how it turned out. I hope you don't mind."

"I would have been glad to show you around,"

Brooke said, trying to keep the anger out of her voice.

"I know, dear, but I had nothing better to do while I waited," Monique said patronizingly, dismissing the subject. She seated herself on one of the high-backed chairs and crossed one leg elegantly over the other, lighting a cigarette and then blowing a large cloud of smoke before she continued. "Actually, I stopped by to see if you'd like to have lunch, but," she glanced at her watch, "it's rather late now. And I do have another appointment. Perhaps another time.

"But I do have a moment to chat. How are things going, Brooke? I realize that all of this must be rather strange for you. I understand your previous social position was...well, no need to bring that up," she laughed, a brief, artificial laugh. "It must be rather difficult to keep someone of Alan's...experience...interested," she said meaningfully, with a glance in the direction of Brooke's bedroom.

Brooke blushed furiously, trying frantically to think of some reply to those barbed remarks.

"Alan seems satisfied," she replied.

"I'm sure he does." The woman reached over and patted Brooke's hand in sympathy. "But if you should ever need any help or advice, please let me know. Alan and I are old...friends...you know."

"Oh?" Despite herself Brooke was encouraging the woman to continue.

"Oh, my, yes!" Monique laughed again and took another long, slow puff on her cigarette. "Alan and I have been very close. In fact, I was quite shocked to learn that he'd married. He and I had sort of an understanding...."

Her voice trailed off and her eyes narrowed, as if a thought had just come to her. "It was a rather hurried wedding. There wasn't any reason that you had to get married, was there?" she asked. Then she added softly, "It would be like Alan to do something gallant."

Brooke looked at the woman, startled. Did she suspect that an important business deal hinged on the marriage? But that was impossible. She was sure Alan had told no one about the true reason for their marriage. So what could Monique have meant by—of course! It was the oldest reason in the world. She rose and tilted her chin up proudly.

"If you know Alan as well as you claim, then I'm sure you know that he could never be forced to do anything he didn't want to do. If you're curious about why he married me, I suggest you ask him."

Monique regarded Brooke thoughtfully for a moment, then stubbed out her cigarette and rose. "Well, my dear, I'm sure he had his reasons." She glanced again toward Brooke's bedroom as she walked toward the hall. "And it would be very interesting to discover them. Very interesting indeed," she added softly, almost to herself.

Brooke watched her leave, a sense of foreboding overtaking her. There was something ruthless, almost sinister, about that woman. Now that she had discovered they were using separate bedrooms, would spite and jealousy make her do something to jeopardize Alan's business deal?

Brooke rose in agitation and began to pace. Should she mention the incident to Alan? He was so unapproachable lately that she shrank at the thought. No doubt he would be displeased. But perhaps nothing would come of it. After all, if Monique didn't know about Alan's business deal, what could she do with the information?

For the next few days Brooke anxiously waited for an explosion, but none came. Apparently Monique didn't know that she possessed damaging information. Or if she did, she was biding her time, waiting to play her trump card at exactly the right moment.

Brooke saw little of Alan during those days, although his light was frequently on late at night. When they did meet he treated her with cool, impersonal

132

courtesy. Suzanne was not very good company, either, with so many housekeeping duties. And although Brooke enjoyed reading and sunbathing by the pool, she soon tired of a steady diet of those activities. She was used to an active life and she enjoyed being with people, and neither need was being met in her present situation.

Finally one morning she decided to take Alan up on his offer to let her use one of the two cars he kept in the garage. A trip to nearby Monaco would be a nice change of pace. She informed Suzanne of her intentions, and though the woman's face registered faint surprise, she only nodded and wished her a pleasant day.

Brooke wasn't familiar with the make of car in Alan's garage, but she quickly adjusted to its idiosyncrasies and was able to enjoy the view around her. The road hugged the semi-mountainous terrain, which fell off sharply to her right. The deep blue sea seemed to stretch to infinity in the distance, and the sunlight on the waves made them sparkle like diamonds.

Brooke took a deep breath and forced herself to relax. The intense strain she'd been under, combined with sleepless nights, was beginning to show. As she drove, the sunshine warm on her skin through the window, she felt the tension draining out of her. Away from the confines of the house, where everything reminded her of Alan, she was able to relax. The relief was tremendous.

Brooke parked near the wharf in Monaco and decided to walk up to the palace. She and Alan had visited the area before, but her knee injury had kept them from really exploring that part of Monaco.

The climb to the top left her breathless, and she paused at the summit to enjoy the view below her. The harbor curved in a deep horseshoe, and the hills rose sharply around it from the sea, the pastel-colored houses clinging precariously to the sides. Yachts of all sizes filled the harbor, and for a moment she recalled the tension of her days on Nick's yacht. A frown crossed her brow, but she determinedly dismissed the thought. Nothing was going to ruin her day, she decided.

She quickened her pace, and soon she was in front of the pinkish-beige palace with its crenulated, stone clock tower. On either side of the ornate entrance gate soldiers in white uniforms stood guard. Although the palace was rather plain on the outside, the setting was fairy-tale-like, and Brooke indulged her romantic fancies for a moment. Then she turned away and spent the next hour or so exploring the tiny shops and sampling some of the French pastries from the little bakeries.

Her stroll led her to a cliff-side path that meandered through well-tended areas of native foliage and offered beautiful views of the Mediterranean. Benches were invitingly and intimately tucked along the walkway. She followed the path almost down to the water and then began retracing her steps, stopping to rest about halfway back at one of the secluded benches.

Closing her eyes, she leaned back, content to savor this respite from the tension of the past few weeks. Two months ago, she had never even heard of Alan d'Aprix. It seemed as if she'd aged years since then. But at least it would be over soon. Much as she loved Alan, she had come to accept the fact that he could never return her love, and the sooner she left, the sooner she would be able to pick up the pieces of her life.

"Hi there. You've found a great spot. Mind if I join you?"

Startled, Brooke opened her eyes and stared at the young man in white across from her. He wore deck shoes and a jaunty yachting cap. His open, freckled face, bright blue eyes, and midwestern accent told her that he was a fellow American. Brooke, starved for companionship, welcomed the intrusion on her thoughts and moved to one side of the bench.

"I'm glad for some company," she told the man. "Besides, it's nice to hear an American. You are from the United States, aren't you?"

"Kansas City," he informed her with a grin. "Is it that obvious? I hoped some of this continental polish would rub off on me," he said with mock disappointment.

"Sorry," Brooke said, laughing.

"That's okay. With this face I'd never pass as the sauve, debonair type anyway. Are you on vacation?" he asked in a friendly tone.

"Yes. No. I mean, I was. Now I'm married."

"Oh." He glanced down at her left hand and gave a soft whistle. "I don't know how I missed that before."

She looked down at the sparkling ring on her finger, knowing that soon it would be gone. With an effort she glanced away and forced herself to smile. "How about you? Are you on vacation?"

"No such luck. I have a job on one of the yachts. I figured that was the only way I'd ever get to see the world. So far it's been working out fine. By the way, my name is Tom Williams."

"It's nice to meet you, Tom. I'm Brooke d'Aprix. Tell me about some of the places you've been," she encouraged with interest.

"Are you sure you want to hear about them? I don't want to bore you."

"You won't, believe me. I haven't traveled that much, and I'm always interested in hearing about new places."

"Okay. I don't need much encouragement. I love to talk." Prompted by Brooke's eager questions, he recounted many of his experiences, amusing her with anecdotes and imitations of various people he'd met. Finally he paused and glanced at his watch.

"Wow! Do you realize that we've been sitting here

for almost two hours? It's way past lunch time."

"Are you late?" Brooke asked with concern. "Do you need to get back to your ship?"

"No. I have the day off. But I'm not used to going this long without food. Would you like to join me for a late lunch? There's a nice cafe on the waterfront."

Brooke hesitated, but only for a moment. "I'd love to. I'm starved."

They made their way down from the palace area back to the harbor level. At one point in their descent Tom stopped to point out the yacht on which he worked. It was similar to Nick's, although not quite as large.

"It's beautiful," Brooke remarked appreciatively. "Do you really enjoy your job?"

"It's great. For now," he amended. "I figure the time to see the world is when you're young, but eventually I want to go home and finish my master's degree in archeology."

"Archeology? I've never known an archeologist before. Tell me about it."

While they ate, he told Brooke about his interest in the field and about a few of the digs he had been on as an undergraduate and as a graduate student. The time flew by, and the sun was already beginning to dip toward the horizon when Brooke realized how late it was. With a start she glanced at her watch.

"Oh my goodness! Look at the time! I didn't realize it was this late!" she exclaimed.

"You're a good listener, and it's not often I get a chance to reminisce with a fellow American. I'm sorry if I've kept you," Tom said apologetically.

"It's all right, but the maid may be wondering where I am." *Alan probably won't even know I was gone,* she added dismally to herself.

"You don't look too happy, Brooke. I have caused a problem, haven't I?"

"No, not at all," she hastened to reassure him. "I've

136

had a wonderful time. It can be awfully lonely living in a foreign country."

Tom frowned and glanced at her ring. He seemed about to make some comment, but then thought better of it and stood up instead. "Well, thanks for a pleasant afternoon. I've enjoyed talking with you."

"Thank you, Tom. It's been fun. I hope you have a lot more exciting experiences in your travels."

"Thanks. Take care now." He grinned and gave her a jaunty salute. Then he turned away and strolled toward the harbor, his cap tilted at a rakish angle. She listened to his gay, whistling tune fade slowly away.

To Brooke he seemed young and carefree, though he probably wasn't any younger than she. Once again she felt old beyond her years. With a sigh, she walked back to the car, unwilling to face another long evening in the silent house above the sea. Beautiful as it was, it was too linked with dreams that could never come true to give her pleasure.

As she drove the winding road back toward Nice, she thought how much everything had changed since that night in Paris. She didn't know if he was angry, had grown tired of the charade, or was regretting it entirely. Maybe it was a combination of all three. In any case, his avoidance of her was all too obvious. He no longer wanted her company.

Even a return to their former friendship now seemed impossible. But perhaps this was best. When she left, it would be a clean break. She would be able to start fresh. In fact, she really should be making plans to leave. Surely the deal would be completed within a few days.

But somehow she couldn't bring herself to do anything. There was something so final about making those arrangements. And much as being near Alan hurt, the thought of leaving and never seeing him again was even worse.

After Brooke put the car away she paused for a moment to look at Alan's home. It really was palatial. And the setting was spectacular. At this moment the house was silhouetted against an orange and yellow sky, and the sinking sun cast a golden path on the darkening sea.

Someday, she supposed, Alan would bring a real bride to live here. *How would he explain this "marriage,"* she wondered, *or would he even consider it important enough to mention?* Tears welled up in her eyes and her throat constricted. She knew that if he ever truly loved, it would be with an intensity that would endure beyond time and space. When—or if—he gave his heart it would not be given lightly and it would be forever. In that sense they were alike. She had given her heart, and she would never again love with the same depth.

She paused on the terrace for another look at the sea, and immediately a shaft of light from an opening door was thrown on the stone surface.

"Madame d'Aprix! Is that you?"

It was Suzanne, and Brooke turned toward the figure outlined in the doorway.

"Yes. I just returned."

"I was beginning to worry," the woman said, the relief evident in her voice. "These roads can be dangerous if one is not used to driving on them."

"I'm fine," Brooke assured her. "Is...is M. d'Aprix home yet?"

"No, madame. Would you like your dinner now?"

"Maybe later. I'm not hungry yet," Brooke said, her voice edged with disappointment. Apparently another day would pass without even a glimpse of Alan.

Wearily Brooke sat on one of the comfortable wicker chairs. She rested her head against the back and closed her eyes. Tomorrow, she resolved, she would make a point to confront Alan and find out the status of the land deal. She couldn't put off that unpleasant task any longer.

Brooke didn't know how long she had been sitting on the terrace, but suddenly another shaft of light was thrown on the stones. Probably Suzanne was coming back to see if she wanted dinner yet.

"I'm still not hungry, Suzanne. I don't think I'll have anything to eat tonight."

"Still full from lunch?"

Brooke's eyes grew wide. She jumped up and turned to face Alan in the doorway, only to find herself caught in the full glare of the light spilling from the opening. She blinked and put her hand up to shield her eyes, but she still couldn't see his face. His voice had been filled with sarcasm, and he stood with feet apart, fists planted firmly on his hips.

Her heart began to thump heavily. He was angry, there was no question about that. Suddenly his question registered, and a cold fear gripped her. Had he found out about her lunch with Tom? And if so, how?

"Wh...what do you mean?" she stammered.

Instead of responding he walked toward her slowly and deliberately. She moved backward, but soon found herself up against the stone wall of the terrace. He continued walking until he was directly in front of her. His mouth was a grim, unsmiling line and his eyes were chips of flinty steel that glittered dangerously. They reflected a leashed violence that made her shudder, and she stared at him in terror.

"I meant exactly what I said. I should think you'd still be full after an afternoon-long lunch with a handsome sailor."

"How did you know?" she whispered.

"Then you admit it?" he demanded.

"Of course, but—"

"Do you realize that you were sitting in plain view at that sidewalk cafe?" he cut in sharply. "Couldn't you have been a bit more discreet? Any one of my friends could have seen you. Don't you think they would wonder why my new wife found it necessary to go

139

elsewhere for entertainment? That would put me in a rather awkward position."

"I...I didn't think of that," she admitted.

"I'm sure you didn't," he said bitterly. "May I ask how long this has been going on?"

"I just met him today," she replied defensively.

"Really?" His sarcastic tone made it clear that he didn't believe her.

"Yes, really!" she shot back, growing angry herself. Maybe she shouldn't have done it, but he didn't have to be so high-handed about the whole thing. After all, it wasn't as if they were really married.

"May I ask why you found it necessary to let a stranger pick you up?"

"I didn't let a stranger 'pick me up'," she declared hotly. "We simply had lunch together. Besides, what do you expect me to do? Sit around here all day and twiddle my thumbs? I was lonely."

For a moment there was silence, and when he spoke again his voice was so soft that it made her shiver. "Well, if it's companionship you wanted, you should have said something sooner."

She looked up at him in alarm, but before she could protest he pulled her roughly toward him and his hard mouth came down on hers in a brutal kiss. Vainly she tried to pull free, but his grip was like iron. The merciless pressure of his mouth intensified, and she struggled to lower her head. In response he gripped the hair that was cascading down her back and pulled sharply, forcing her head back up. Her low moan was stifled as his lips once more came down on hers.

There was no love or gentleness in Alan's kiss, only a desire to hurt. But despite that fact, she discovered that her senses had leapt to life at his touch. Her reaction disgusted her. She should hate him. Instead, she found herself wanting the embrace to continue, even though it was cruelly inflicted. She knew she should keep up her struggle, but finally she gave up. She couldn't escape, and her traitorous body was his ally.

Sensing her change from resistance to submission, Alan suddenly lifted his lips from hers and stared down into her eyes. Mutely she returned his look. For the first time he seemed to realize what he'd done. She heard him swear softly under his breath as he abruptly let her go and stepped back.

For a moment she thought she was going to fall, but she gripped the back of the chair next to her to steady herself. For a long moment Alan stared at her in the darkness, and then without a word he turned and went inside.

Shakily Brooke sank into a convenient chair, her breath coming in uneven gasps. She put her face into her trembling hands, careful not to touch her bruised lips, and before she could stop it a ragged sob escaped from her throat. Then another came, and before long she was crying in the darkness, the tears streaming down her face. All the tension of the last few weeks was suddenly flooding out.

When at last her tears ceased, she felt better and more composed than she had in a long time. After this incident Alan certainly couldn't expect her to honor their agreement. It wasn't just that he had violated it again, although that was reason enough. In her heart Brooke knew that she could no longer keep her feelings a secret from the man whose love she so desperately wanted.

Tomorrow she would leave. When he got home, she would be gone.

For the first time since she'd lived with Alan, Brooke locked her door before she went to bed.

# Chapter Twelve

The sun was just coming up when Brooke finally went to sleep, and as a result, Alan, as always, was gone when she awakened. She rose and dressed quickly, and though she applied her makeup with a heavier hand than usual, it could not hide the havoc that the last few weeks had wrought in her features. Her eyelids were puffy and red, fine lines had appeared around her eyes, and her complexion was pale. Finally she gave up the attempt to make herself look presentable. No one would see her anyway.

Brooke spent most of the morning making flight arrangements. She discovered that there wouldn't be another direct flight to London until the next morning, so she opted for two short, connecting flights. She knew that she could not spend another night under this roof.

Next she called Mary, who, though surprised, told her that her old room was still vacant. "I haven't been able to find another suitable roommate," she lamented. "So of course you're welcome!"

Brooke knew Mary was dying to ask questions, but her friend restrained herself, and Brooke silently thanked her. There would be time for explanations later.

After arranging for Jacques to drive her to the airport, only the packing was left. She opened the closet in her bedroom and surveyed the beautiful clothes regretfully, fingering the filmy blue dress she'd worn at the reception. Then, resolutely, she closed the door. She would take only the essentials. She wanted to feel under no obligation to Alan.

As she packed, the flash of her diamond ring caught her eye, and she paused for a moment to look at it. Though she'd known all along that the ring was only hers for a short time, she had dreaded the moment when she must remove it. In her mind, that would be the final sign of the relationship's end, even if it was still in effect on paper.

But the time had come. With a deep breath she pulled it off, cradling it for a moment in her hand. Then she set it on the dressing table, next to the notepaper on which she intended to inform Alan of her departure. Writing that note was one of the things she least relished, so she put it off until last.

Slowly and methodically she packed her toilet articles. When she was finished she carried the small case into the living room, intending to leave it there for Jacques. As she passed through the hall the doorbell rang, and she paused.

"I'll get it, Suzanne," she called.

Brooke opened the door and stared in surprise at the fashionably dressed woman standing before her.

"Monique!"

"Hello, Brooke." The woman's eyes quickly took in Brooke's devastated face and the suitcase in her hand. "Am I interrupting anything?"

"No, not at all."

"Good. May I come in, then?" Without waiting for a reply, she strolled into the drawing room. Brooke followed her and set the small suitcase down as unobtrusively as possible next to the couch.

"Are you and Alan planning another trip?" Monique asked brightly, her eyes hard.

144

"No. I'm going to visit a friend."

"How nice. It must get lonely up here, with Alan working such long hours. By the way, did you have a nice lunch yesterday?" she asked innocently.

Brooke stared at her.

"Lunch?"

"Yes. I saw you with that nice-looking sailor as I drove by. Wherever did you find such a good-looking man?"

So that was how Alan had found out about it!

"He was just someone I ran into while I was visiting Monaco," Brooke said stiffly.

"Well, some of us are more lucky than others," Monique sighed in an affected manner. Then she adopted a serious tone. "Brooke, may I be frank with you for a moment?"

Brooke was sure she didn't want to hear anything Monique would have to say, but she hoped that if she listened Monique would leave quickly. There was more packing to do before time to go to the airport.

"Certainly."

"Now stop me if I'm wrong, but let me tell you how I see the situation between you and Alan at the moment. First of all, I'm sure you realize that you're out of your element here. And Alan must realize it, too. I don't know what prompted him to run off and marry in such a hurry. Obviously he needed a wife for some reason. Why, I don't know," she admitted thoughtfully as she drew out a cigarette and paused to light it.

"But that's beside the point. If I hadn't decided to travel to Italy, Alan would have called on me for assistance, I'm sure. And I would have been more than happy to oblige. After all, everyone assumed that we'd marry eventually, anyway."

She looked over at Brooke as if to gauge the other woman's reaction, but Brooke kept her face expressionless.

"Well, apparently none of this is news to you. Let's

be honest, dear. You're simply not Alan's type."

*But you are, I suppose*, Brooke thought bitterly.

"When I saw you with the suitcase," Monique continued, "I thought perhaps you'd realized that, too. Maybe you have. It's quite obvious that you love Alan, and I know how hard it must be for you to admit that the marriage was a mistake. But surely it's been apparent to you for some time." She glanced toward Brooke's bedroom, and Brooke's color rose.

"I really don't see how any of this has—" Brooke began, but Monique cut her off.

"Naturally I don't want to interfere. Don't misunderstand. And I'm sure we both want what's best for Alan. That's all I ask you to think about—if you haven't already." She glanced at the suitcase and stood up. "Well, dear, I'll let myself out. Have a nice trip."

Brooke remained where she sat, too numb to move. She wasn't really surprised. She'd suspected for some time that there had been more to Monique and Alan's relationship than Alan had admitted. Monique had now confirmed that. *Well, he can soon have her permanently, if that's what he wants*, she thought wearily. After today, she would be out of his life forever.

At Suzanne's insistence, Brooke ate a light lunch and then went back to her bedroom to finish packing. She was only taking one suitcase in addition to her overnight case, but the job took longer than she thought because she went about it so listlessly. Halfway through she paused to dress for the trip, donning a simple gray circular skirt and a long-sleeved silk blouse. As she buckled her belt she was conscious of the fact that she'd lost weight, but she didn't really care.

Finally she snapped the suitcase shut and turned toward the desk on which the sheet of notepaper lay expectantly. Now came the hardest part. What was she going to say? With all her heart she longed to tell Alan how she really felt, but she knew that would be un-

146

wise. The best thing to do was to keep it short and simple.

She had just written "Alan" across the top of the sheet when she felt a faint prickling sensation at the back of her neck. She had inadvertently left her bedroom door open during the last stage of her packing, and now she instinctively knew that Alan was standing on the threshold. Slowly she turned and stood up. She had hoped to avoid a confrontation, but now she was just going to have to face it.

For the first time in their relationship it was she who was poised and he who seemed uncertain. He looked strained and tense as he stood in the doorway, holding a bouquet of exquisite coral roses just like the ones he had bought for her in the flower market. Brooke looked at him in surprise, waiting for him to make the first move. He cleared his throat, and when he spoke his voice was strangely tight.

"I've come to apologize for last night, Brooke. I don't know if you can ever forgive me. My actions were totally uncalled for. I hope you'll accept these as a peace offering." He held the roses out to her, and she took them silently, breathing deeply of their fragrance. She was extremely touched by the gesture, for she knew Alan did not often humble himself in this way. It made what she had to say all the more difficult.

"Thank you, Alan. They're beautiful." She took another whiff and then laid them on the desk. "But I hope you'll understand when I tell you that I can't stay any longer. Things have just deteriorated to the point where I can't continue with the charade. I hope this won't affect your land deal."

"No," he said with a resigned sigh. "The deal has been concluded. Favorably."

"I'm glad." Why hadn't he told her that before? "Then it won't matter if I leave."

He seemed about to reply, but then changed his mind.

"I've made all the flight arrangements. Jacques is driving me to the airport in about an hour."

"Today? You're leaving today?" He seemed stunned.

"Yes."

He glanced toward the bed and for the first time seemed aware of the suitcase on top of it. "I guess there really isn't anything to keep you here any longer." It was a statement, made in a flat voice that revealed no emotion. Brooke was surprised at the tone, though, for she had expected him to greet her news with pleasure. He would be free to pursue Monique, which surely was what he wanted to do. Monique had practically said as much.

"No. Our business is finished. You'll…see to all of the legalities?" She couldn't bring herself to say the word *annulment*.

"Of course." He fixed his intense eyes on her and she looked away, afraid that he might read her true feelings in her eyes.

"I'll leave the address where I can be reached." She picked up the pen and hastily scribbled Mary's London address. "I'll be there until I leave for the States," she said, handing him the paper.

He took it silently and stared at the address, a frown on his face. When he made no comment, Brooke replaced the pen on the desk and walked over to her suitcase.

"I'd better be going. Jacques will want to load my luggage in the car."

Alan folded the slip of paper and placed it in his breast pocket. "I'll drive you."

Brooke turned to him, startled. She hadn't expected the offer, and she desperately tried to think of a way to refuse. She didn't want to prolong this scene. But Alan didn't give her a chance to speak. He was beside her in one easy stride and effortlessly lifted the suitcase.

"Is this all?"

"My overnight case is in the drawing room. This

148

isn't really necessary, Alan. Jacques is planning to take me to the airport."

"I'm going that direction anyway. Might as well save him a trip."

Brooke gave up. Alan was obviously determined to take her, and if he could put up with the awkward situation, she could, too.

"Where's your other case?" he asked as they entered the drawing room.

"By the settee. I can get it."

He ignored her and picked it up, too, tucking it under one arm.

"This can't be all of your luggage," he frowned.

"I've taken everything I need. I really won't have any use for the evening gowns or cocktail dresses. I have a feeling they won't fit into the lifestyle I'm going back to."

"That's ridiculous," Alan said impatiently. "Certainly you'll have more use for them than I will. What do you think I'm going to do with them?"

"I've only worn some of them once. Maybe Madame Barry would be willing to take them back," she suggested.

In response he simply sent her a dark look, so she made no further comment. The clothes were his problem, after all.

As Brooke had feared, the ride to the airport was a silent, strained one. Although she tried to concentrate on the scenery and enjoy her last view of the Riviera, it was impossible. She was all too conscious of the man beside her and of the fact that this was the last time she would ever sit next to him. Tears rose behind her eyes and she bit her lip to keep them from spilling out. She mustn't let him see how she really felt about leaving. He would just think her a lovesick schoolgirl, and she wouldn't be able to bear that.

She finally admitted to herself that almost from the beginning she had harbored a secret hope that he

149

would come to love her as she loved him. It had been foolish, she now knew. How could she ever hope to compete with someone of Monique's experience and sophistication? The woman had been right. Brooke was out of her element in Alan's world.

As the airport came into sight, Brooke closed her eyes and gave silent thanks. She couldn't bear to be with Alan another minute in this atmosphere. Much as she dreaded the thought of leaving him, it was better than being physically with him but mentally and spiritually alone.

Brooke was out of the car and waiting by the trunk almost before Alan had stopped. When he joined her he gave a bitter smile. "You are anxious to leave, aren't you?"

"Well, I don't want to miss my plane," she replied lamely. "I can handle those, Alan," she said as he removed her suitcases. "I don't want to keep you from anything."

"You aren't. I kept the afternoon free. I had hoped we could have lunch and talk things over." He glanced around the parking lot ruefully. "This spot isn't exactly conducive to discussion. What time does your flight leave?"

"Four o'clock."

"We have time for a quick snack before that," he said, glancing at his watch. "Would you mind, Brooke? I don't want you to leave on this note. I wish we could at least be friends."

Brooke sighed inwardly. She couldn't doubt the sincerity in his voice and she couldn't resist his persuasive tone. At heart Alan was thoughtful, sensitive, and charming, and the demise of their relationship was perhaps as much her fault as his.

"I guess I have a few minutes," she agreed, and was rewarded by one of his warm smiles—a smile she hadn't seen for some time.

Once she had checked in and deposited her luggage,

Alan took her to a quiet cafe. It reminded her of their days in Paris, and she smiled.

"A penny for them." Alan smiled at her. Luckily, she was saved from having to answer by the appearance of a waiter. "Brooke?" Alan asked.

"Just something to drink, please."

Alan gave their order and then turned to her.

"Well, Brooke, I think I owe you an explanation for my behavior during these past weeks."

"Oh, no, Alan, really you don't," she protested. She didn't want to listen to any explanations about his growing weary of the charade and his longing to be free so that he could be with Monique. "It doesn't matter. I understand. And now that the business is concluded, I'm leaving. It's as simple as that. It's what we agreed."

"Yes," he nodded. "I had hoped..." His voice trailed off. "Brooke, answer just one question. Is that all it was to you—strictly a business deal?"

His eyes burned into hers, with such intensity that she lowered her eyelids. She had to convince him that he wasn't sending her off with a broken heart.

"Of course. You did me a favor, and I did one for you. Now it's over and we both can go on with our lives." She was lying, and she prayed that for once he wouldn't be able to read her true thoughts.

"I see." He fingered the glass the waiter had set in front of him, his brooding eyes fixed on the liquid inside. At last he lifted his glass. "Well, I guess the only thing left to do is drink to the future."

Brooke looked at him, a question in her eyes. His voice held a note of—what was it, she wondered? Disappointment? Impossible! Was she imagining things? She had assumed that he would be so happy....

"Well, well, well. What a coincidence!"

Brooke looked up at the familiar voice, her glass halfway to her lips.

151

"Monique! What a surprise. Will you join us?" Alan asked politely.

"Oh, no, dear. I have lots of shopping to do today. But I thought I saw the two of you sitting here, and I had to come over and say hello. Ready for your trip, Brooke?"

"Yes. I'll be leaving in a few minutes," Brooke replied tonelessly.

"Well, you must have a lovely time!" Monique said gaily.

"How did you know that Brooke was leaving?" Alan asked tersely, his voice sharp.

"Oh, now, don't get all huffy, Alan, dear. I stopped by the house this morning to see if Brooke wanted to have lunch and caught her in the middle of packing. You said you were going to visit a friend, I believe?"

"Yes," Brooke nodded, noting the look of relief on Alan's face. Did he really think that she would tell Monique the real reason for her departure without first consulting him? He didn't have much faith in her, it seemed.

"Well, I won't keep you. I wouldn't want you to miss your plane. But Alan," Monique turned her attention to him, "I do have a great favor to ask. I simply must attend an art show opening next week, and positively everyone I wanted to ask is out of town. Would you be a dear and accompany me? Brooke, you wouldn't mind, would you? It's purely a social affair." Monique smiled at her brightly.

*It's not taking her much time to move in*, Brooke noted.

"No, of course not. Alan can do whatever he likes." She looked up at him and found him watching her. A sob rose in her throat and she quickly turned away.

"Well, as long as my wife doesn't mind, I'd be delighted." He smiled charmingly down at Monique and she linked her arm in his and leaned close to him.

"Wonderful! We can work out all the details later.

I'm sure Brooke is anxious to leave." She reached up and kissed Alan lightly on the cheek. "Until next week, darling. Brooke, you have a very nice trip. Au revoir." She waved gaily and strolled down the street. Alan sat down again, but he made no attempt at conversation. At last, to break the heavy silence, Brooke spoke.

"Well, Alan, I guess we better leave. My plane will be taking off shortly."

"All right." He took a last swallow of his drink and stood up.

Brooke arrived at her gate just in time to board the plane, and for that she was thankful. She really didn't know what else to say to Alan. She turned to him and summoned up a tremulous smile.

"I guess this is good-bye. It's been a very...interesting experience. Thank you for all your hospitality." The words sounded stiff even to her, but he seemed equally at a loss as to how to end their relationship.

"Brooke, I—"

"Last call for flight 903. All passengers should be aboard the aircraft." The booming voice from the loudspeaker cut him off, and Brooke didn't give him a chance to finish his sentence.

"Take care, Alan," she called over her shoulder as she ran toward the gate. She turned back once before she entered the ramp, unable to resist a last glimpse of him. He was standing just the way she'd seen him that first day as she was being put in the ambulance. His jacket was open, and one hand was in the pocket of his slacks in an achingly familiar pose.

When he realized that she was looking at him he raised one hand briefly in a salute, but he didn't smile. Brooke turned away, stumbling as tears clouded her vision.

"Are you all right, miss?" an attendant asked in a worried voice.

"Yes, thank you. I must have gotten something in

153

my eye. I'll be fine," said Brooke.

But in her heart, she didn't know if she would ever be fine again.

# Chapter Thirteen

Mary was waiting at their London flat to greet Brooke with a warm hug and much fussing. But she didn't ask Brooke about anything that had happened, and Brooke didn't offer any explanations.

"Your room is all ready," she said. "Why don't you go in and freshen up and we'll eat dinner in a little while."

"Okay. Thanks, Mary."

The small room with the chintz-covered bed was just as she'd left it a few weeks ago—or was it a lifetime? In many ways, it was as though she'd never left. Perhaps these last few weeks really had been simply a dream, and now she was awake. Everything about her life with Alan had a dream-like quality—the beautiful clothes, the villa, the cruise on Nick's yacht, the honeymoon in Paris. Had all those things been real?

"Did you have a nice flight?" Mary asked as they sat down to a dinner of boiled beef with potatoes and English peas. "By the way, I'm sorry dinner isn't a bit more elaborate. But you took me by surprise."

"This is fine," Brooke assured her friend. She wasn't hungry, but she made an effort to eat a few mouthfuls so she wouldn't hurt Mary's feelings. "How is your father?"

"Just fine," Mary told her. "He gave us quite a scare,

but he's back to normal now. It's too bad it had to happen during our trip though. Just think, if I'd stayed, maybe I'd have met a millionaire, too!" At once Mary realized the inappropriateness of her comment and her face fell. "Oh, Brooke, I'm so sorry! I was determined not to bring that up unless you did."

"It's all right, Mary," Brooke sighed. "You deserve some sort of explanation, considering the fact that I dropped in on you so unexpectedly."

"No, love, you don't have to say a thing if you don't want to."

"Well, I don't think I'm ready to talk about all the details yet, but I'll give you the gist of what happened." So Brooke told Mary about her accident, Alan d'Aprix's offer, her recuperation at his house and his business proposition. "I really felt it was the least I could do for him, considering how kind he'd been to me," Brooke finished. "And of course, now that the deal is completed, my role is over. So I left. That's the story—an abbreviated version, I admit—but you've got all the facts."

"Except one, I think," Mary said quietly. "You fell in love with Alan d'Aprix, didn't you?"

Brooke looked down at her barely touched food and felt the tears forming behind her eyes. It wouldn't do any good to lie to Mary. They had been friends for too long. "It's my own fault. I knew from the start that I was being foolish. I guess I just hoped that he would fall in love with me, too. It was a silly fantasy."

"Why was it so silly?" Mary asked indignantly. "You're a warm, loving person. Any man would be a fool to pass up the chance to marry you."

Brooke forced herself to grin as she wiped her eyes with a tissue. "Thanks for the compliment, Mary."

"Well, it's true. Is he crazy? Why would he pass up an opportunity to ask you to be his real wife?"

"There's someone else," Brooke said quietly.

"Oh." For a moment Mary was silent. "Well, she

couldn't have been nicer than you are. Is she a social-ite type?"

"Something like that."

"I still say he's a fool to want her when he could have you," Mary said stubbornly as she rose to clear the table.

"Oh, I don't know," Brooke said with resignation as she, too, rose and gathered up the silverware. "She comes from the same social circle as Alan. They have the same kind of background and lifestyle. Maybe I would have been out of place."

Mary gave an unladylike snort. "I don't believe that for a minute. But you're probably better off without him. If he didn't realize what he had in you, he's not worth having."

"Thanks for the vote of confidence," Brooke said with a wry smile. Mary's common-sense approach to life was just what Brooke needed right now.

"It's good to have you back, love," Mary said. "What are you planning to do now?"

"I think I'll stay in London for a while, if you can put up with me, and see if I can find a job at a museum, or maybe as a teacher."

"Of course you're welcome to stay," Mary assured her. "The room is still available for as long as you need it. Any idea how long you'll stay?"

"Oh, I don't know," Brooke said vaguely. "I guess it depends on what kind of job I get. If I find an interesting job, I might stay another year or so." Maybe by then her love for Alan would dim and she would be ready to plan a new life. "I'm not promising anything, though. I gave Alan this address, so he'll be sending all the papers here. Once that business is cleared up, I may decide to leave."

"Of course. You have to do whatever you think best."

For the next week Brooke spent her time compiling a résumé and submitting it to all of the likely prospects. When she wasn't out job hunting, she cleaned the apartment from top to bottom, exhausting herself physically so that by the time she fell into bed at night she could sleep.

Nights were the worst, for the few times she found sleep elusive, her thoughts inevitably turned to Alan. She found herself wondering what he was doing at that particular moment, and invariably Monique came to mind. Then she would toss and turn for hours and get up in the morning looking more tired than when she'd gone to bed.

At last she began to get some responses to her résumés, and one job particularly intrigued her. It was the position of assistant curator in a small museum that specialized in artifacts from the Middle Ages. The job sounded exactly like something she would enjoy. She called and set up an interview.

When Brooke arrived at the museum later that week she was greeted by a young woman who smiled apologetically. "I'm afraid Mr. Smythe, the curator, was called out unexpectedly. But he should be back at any time, Miss Peyton. Would you mind waiting?"

"No, not at all," Brooke replied. Actually she was rather glad for some time to compose herself. She was nervous about the interview and wanted to make a good impression.

"You aren't English, are you?" the young woman asked her curiously.

"No," Brooke admitted with a smile. "But English history was my specialty in graduate school."

"Yes, Mr. Smythe mentioned that. He was very impressed with your résumé."

"Well, maybe that's a good omen." Brooke glanced around the small office. The museum was located in an older building, and various artifacts hung on the wall even in this outer office.

She had only had a quick glimpse of the museum display on her way to the office, but she had liked what she'd seen. Items were arranged simply, and there was no overcrowding as there was in many museums. Each artifact was alone, or grouped with related items, and large printed cards offered explanations. The layout was crisp and clean and conducive to leisurely browsing. She was surprised that she had never heard about the museum while she was in school, and mentioned it to the receptionist.

"Oh, we've only been here about a year," she explained. "In fact, we're still in the process of setting up some of the exhibits. That's where Mr. Smythe is now, actually. He got a tip about an item that would be perfect for a new display he's working on. And he can't pass up a chance like that."

"I don't blame him," Brooke said with a smile. She was beginning to look forward to meeting the curator.

"I'm back, Ann. What good fortune! Indeed, I can't believe the luck! I'm sure—oh. Hello there. You must be Brooke Peyton. I'm Winston Smythe."

He smiled engagingly and held out his hand. His mop of white hair fell in an unruly fashion about his lined face, and Brooke guessed him to be at least sixty years of age. But his pale blue eyes had a youthful sparkle, and a vital energy radiated from him.

He was dressed haphazardly, with only an indifferent concession to propriety. Although he had on a brown suit, his tie was askew and he wore argyle socks with tennis shoes. Brooke was immediately captivated by his infectious good humor and enthusiasm.

She rose and extended her hand. "How do you do, Mr. Smythe. I'm pleased to meet you."

"Thank you. Likewise. Sorry to keep you waiting, but I've just made the most remarkable purchase …well, we can discuss that later. Please come in and we'll talk."

Brooke was ushered into an office that was the antithesis of the orderly, well-designed display rooms she'd seen earlier. Books and papers were piled neck high on the desk, and more papers were similarly arranged on a long work table against one wall and on several chairs in the room. Suddenly realizing that there was nowhere for Brooke to sit, the older man began clearing off one of the chairs, stacking the papers against one of the book-lined walls.

"There you are," he said with satisfaction as he removed the last pile. "Please sit down." He then proceeded to clear a space on the desk so that he could see her. "Quite a mess, isn't it?" he admitted ruefully as he looked around. "I must clean all of this up one day," he added absently. Then he dismissed the subject and turned his attention to Brooke. "Well, now, what can I do for you?"

Brooke looked at him in surprise. "I'm here to be interviewed for the job," she reminded him, struggling to hide a smile.

"Of course, of course. Let me see, I have your application here somewhere." He began to shuffle the papers on the desk, at last pulling one out triumphantly. "Here we are. Yes, yes, now I remember. Well, the job consists of helping me set up new exhibits, doing research—you know, typical museum duties. Does it interest you?"

"Yes, very much. I'm afraid I'm not very experienced, but I learn quickly."

"Experience," he waved her comment aside. "You can get all the experience you'll need right here. Personally, I think prior experience is highly overrated. If a person is smart, he or she can pick things up quite rapidly. And you strike me as being a very intelligent woman."

"Thank you," she replied with a smile. "I'll give it my best. I'm still not exactly sure what duties the job entails, but I love history."

"That's the most important prerequisite," he said. "A love of history. Brooke—may I call you that?"

"Please."

"And you must call me Winston. Can you start Monday?"

"You mean I have the job?" she asked, surprised at the shortness of the interview.

"If you want it. I've reviewed your academic qualifications, and now that I've met you I'm sure you'll do well here. I always wait until I meet a person, no matter how good they look on paper. Personal impressions are very important. Very important indeed. You'll be dealing with the public, and possibly doing some traveling to locate objects for exhibits, and a good personality is a must. I'm afraid I do better here among my books and in the museum than I do with people. Believe it or not, some people think I'm eccentric!" He gave her a solemn wink, but his eyes were twinkling. "As for salary, it's quite reasonable." He mentioned a figure, and Brooke nodded.

"That sounds fine."

"Good. Now, would you like a tour of the museum, or would you rather wait until Monday?"

"I'd like to look around now, if I may. I only got a quick look as I came in."

Winston showed her the various exhibits, pointing out especially interesting objects here and there. The museum covered three floors, and as they stepped out onto the third floor he paused.

"We're still in the process of finishing the exhibits, so only half the floor is open to the public," he explained. "Part of your job will be to help me find artifacts for use in the remaining exhibits." He showed her around the unfinished floor and then led her back to the entrance.

"As you can see, there's still a great deal of work to be done. But we've made tremendous progress. Does the job still interest you?"

"More than ever," she assured him. She was truly looking forward to it, not only because it would take her mind off of Alan, but also because the work sounded fascinating.

"Oh, you'll also be giving tours to special groups. You do like to mingle with people, don't you?"

"Very much."

"I thought so. Well then, Brooke, until Monday."

"Until Monday," she agreed with a smile. "And thank you."

For the next few weeks Brooke plunged into her work with an eagerness that both astonished and pleased Winston.

"I knew you'd be dedicated, but I never expected you to become this involved," he told her one night as they worked late to finish a new exhibit. She knew he was pleased that she had entered into the work so enthusiastically, and that, in turn, pleased her. He was a joy to work for, and his love of history was contagious. He gave her minimal instructions, allowing her to work at her own speed and in her own style. Brooke reveled in the responsibility and sense of accomplishment.

"Brooke," Winston told her another time, "I know you love your work, but you musn't let it become your whole life. You work late almost every night. A pretty young woman like you should be out socializing, too. I don't want this job to damage your personal life."

"Don't worry," she told him with a smile. "I appreciate your concern, but I'm not giving anything up by staying late. I enjoy it. Besides," she teased gently, "you aren't exactly the one to tell me not to make my job my whole life."

"Well, that's different," he told her. "I'm an old man. Too old for all the running around that young people do. But I had my day. Yes indeed," he smiled wistfully. "I had many good times when I was young. I just don't want you to miss that."

"Believe me, I'm not missing anything. For right

now, I want to devote myself to my work. I really do, Winston," she insisted.

"Well, you know best, my dear," he sighed. "Of course, I'm delighted that you love your job."

Brooke did love her job, and she and Winston had developed an immediate sense of camaraderie. But she was not yet ready to share with him her other reason for occupying herself so completely with her work. She had never spoken to anyone except Mary about her marriage to Alan. That was a secret she was unwilling to share with him—or anyone else—yet.

But despite the long hours at her job, there were inevitably times when her thoughts turned to Alan. Sometimes as she lay in bed his image came to her in the dark, and she could picture him in her mind as clearly as if she'd seen him only the day before—his dark hair, lean good looks, and the gentle touch of his hands as they'd helped her during the first difficult days after the accident. His eyes were the clearest feature in her memory—eyes that could be intense and penetrating but at other times so warm that you could almost melt in their gaze.

How she missed him! Somehow the bad times had faded in her memory, and she remembered most clearly the happy moments. Those first days of her recuperation, the intimate dinners on the terrace, their "honeymoon" in Paris—those were the memories that she would treasure forever.

But the most vivid and painful of her memories was the lingering feel of his lips on hers. She could close her eyes and almost believe for a moment that he was near. At those times her heart ached anew, and she wondered if she would ever recover from the sense of loss and pain her love for Alan had caused.

Brooke watched the mail daily for the arrival of legal documents from Alan or his lawyers, and within a couple of weeks of her return a letter with Alan's return address appeared. She opened it with dread, expecting to find annulment papers, but instead the envelope contained only a sheet of writing paper and a check. Her eyes quickly scanned the familiar writing.

Brooke:
You left so suddenly that we didn't have time to discuss a financial settlement. So I have taken the liberty of deciding on a sum, which I will send you each month. If this is not agreeable, please let me know.

Alan

Brooke looked at the check without interest, noting the generous sum, before she put it into a clean envelope and addressed it to Alan. She had never intended to accept money from him after her role ended.

She continued to watch the mail for annulment papers, but the days turned into weeks and nothing came. She didn't understand why he was waiting to file the necessary papers, but perhaps it just took longer than she thought. She had no experience with such matters. Checks, though, continued to appear each month, and Brooke returned those unopened, marked "refused."

She was returning home from work late one afternoon when she stopped on impulse at a newsstand to buy an evening paper. Mary usually picked one up on her way home from work, but she was out of town for a few days visiting her parents.

As Brooke waited for the vendor to make change, her eyes roamed aimlessly over the stand, which was covered from top to bottom with magazines and newspapers of all types. The majority of the publications were gossip sheets of one type or another. Her eyes skimmed the sensational headlines and she smiled to herself. *Did people actually buy these, she wondered? How could anyone believe—*

Her eyes became riveted to one of the papers and the smile froze on her lips. Almost the entire cover was filled with a huge picture of Alan. It took a moment for her to realize that the woman on his arm in the picture was Monique. Only then did she read the headline: "Riviera Tycoon and Heiress to Wed?" it screamed in huge type.

Brooke's vision blurred. She grasped the edge of the wooden stand to steady herself, but the world tilted crazily and she felt blackness engulfing her.

## Chapter Fourteen

"Say, miss, are you all right?"

Brooke fought the blackness, gripping the edge of the stand more tightly. Finally the concerned face of the elderly man behind the counter came into focus.

"Yes. I...I'd like a copy of that paper, please," she said, indicating the one with Alan's picture on the cover. He reached up and removed it, pausing a moment to look at it as he did so.

"Well, looks like another society wedding. Wonder if I'll be invited?" he said jovially. "Handsome bloke, he is. And she's a real looker, too, if you don't mind my sayin' so," he remarked as Brooke handed him the money and tucked the paper in her purse. "Say, miss, are you sure you're all right?"

Brooke nodded and turned away from the stand quickly, her breathing jerky. She had to get control of herself. Wasn't this what she'd expected all along? Why was she reacting so violently? It had been...how long now...eight months since she'd left. Surely she should be in better control of her emotions by now.

Angrily she brushed at the tears threatening to escape from the corners of her eyes, aware that passersby were staring at her. She had to compose herself. Desperately she looked around, and spotting a bench tucked in between two bushes, headed in that direction. She sank onto it dejectedly and for a few moments sat without moving. She loved Alan desperately and knew she always would. Maybe the hurt would eventually lessen, but it would never go away. She was just going to have to accept that.

She started to remove the paper from her purse and then paused. She ought to throw it in the trash can next to the bench. Wasn't she the one who a few minutes ago had been laughing at people who read these scandal sheets? But after all these months, Brooke was hungry for any information about Alan, and against her better judgment she unfolded the paper.

She studied the picture on the cover carefully. The dear, familiar face smiled out at her from the page, just as she remembered it. Well, not quite, she decided as she scrutinized the photo. His face looked thinner and the fine lines around his eyes looked deeper. He'd probably been working too hard.

She looked at Alan's picture for a long time to impress every detail in her memory, and then she turned her attention to Monique. She, too, was smiling a rather smug smile, Brooke thought. Her arm was linked in Alan's, and his right hand covered hers. It was a tender, intimate gesture that tore at Brooke's heart.

As usual, Monique looked stunning. She was dressed in a strapless gown, and Alan wore a tuxedo, so the photo must have been taken at a formal affair. Brooke's eyes dropped to the cutline, which confirmed her guess. It had been snapped at a charity gala in Monaco, and the reader was requested to turn to an inside page for the story.

Brooke did so, hastily scanning the headlines until she found the one she wanted. Then, taking a deep breath, she began to read.

Are wedding bells about to ring for Alan d'Aprix, the wealthy hotel owner, and Monique

Chere, socialite heiress? The two have been constant companions for the last few months, leading many to speculate that wedding plans will soon be announced.

The story went on to discuss Alan's various business enterprises and Monique's charitable and social involvements, and then returned to the subject of the marriage.

Sources say that the two long-time companions are an ideal couple, and it is only a matter of time before they will walk down the aisle.

Perhaps d'Aprix is a bit gun-shy since his brief marriage about a year ago to Brooke Peyton, an American, which took place after a whirlwind courtship. Although he refuses to comment on the status of that marriage, it is apparent that the two have separated. No address is available for Miss Peyton, but she is thought to be currently living in England.

Slowly Brooke closed the paper and leaned back on the bench. She had never expected to find her own name in the article. Why had Alan refused to comment on their marriage?

Carefully she tucked the paper back into her purse and walked home. She felt drained and tired, and she picked listlessly at the simple supper that she fixed for herself. The quiet of the apartment was oppressive. She would be glad when Mary returned.

By the time her roommate did arrive, Brooke had come down with a nasty cold, and at her friend's insistence she called in sick to work. Winston was very solicitous and told her to take as much time as she needed to recover, but she hated to stay home. Sitting around the apartment all day only gave her more time to think about Alan and Monique. She got out the gos-

sip sheet several times and reread the article, each tim
putting it down with the same sick feeling.

Mary fixed her hot soup and light meals an
watched over her like a mother hen. In two day
Brooke felt well enough to go back to work.

"Brooke, you've got to take better care of yourself,
Mary admonished her when her friend was feeling be
ter. "Your resistance is much too low. You don't ea
enough, and you work far too hard."

"I appreciate your concern, Mary. But I feel muc
better now, thanks to you."

"You're too run down," Mary shook her head wor
riedly as she straightened up the living room. "Say
what's this?"

Brooke looked up in alarm, suddenly realizing tha
she'd left the paper with the story about Alan in th
living room. It was too late now, though, because Mar
had already read the headline.

"Oh, Brooke, I'm sorry," she said softly, sittin
down beside her friend. "I knew you were feeling es
pecially low for the last few days, but I just assumed i
was because you were sick."

Brooke covered her face with her hands.

"I just don't know what to do, Mary. I can't ge
through the rest of my life wanting something I ca
never have. I've got to get over this, and I thought
was making progress. Then I saw this at a newsstand,"
she motioned toward the paper, "and it was as if I'c
just left Alan yesterday. I've got to stop loving him or i
will ruin my life. But how, when even a fuzzy photo
graph can reduce me to tears?"

"Oh, love, I know it's been hard for you," said Mary
drawing Brooke close and hugging her.

"But you're a survivor, Brooke. Eventually you'l
put things in perspective again and go on living. You
love life too much to ever let anything keep you dowr
for very long."

"I hope you're right, Mary," Brooke sighed, unconvinced.

Mary's concern was equaled by Winston's. He commented more than once on her run-down appearance, and began to insist that she go home when the museum closed. She was touched by his worry, but the last thing she wanted was more time alone. So she just smiled and compromised by leaving earlier than she had in the past.

One night, as she was preparing to leave, he beckoned to her from his office.

"Can you come in for a moment before you leave, Brooke? I'll just keep you a short time."

"Certainly," she said, depositing her coat and purse on a chair in the outer office as she followed him inside. He seated himself at his desk and searched through the stacks of papers until he found what he wanted. He scanned the document for a moment and then handed it to her.

"It seems there's an antique dealer in Paris who has made a lucky purchase. A real artifact from the twelfth century. Thank heavens he had the good sense to call an expert and have it authenticated. Anyway, it sounds like it may be just what we need to complete our exhibit on the third floor. Obviously we could have it shipped, but I hate to take chances with a fragile object of this nature. I'd feel much better if we hand-carried it back here. Would you mind going to Paris and picking it up, Brooke? At the same time you can make sure that its condition is as good as this photo indicates before we conclude the purchase."

Paris! The very thought of returning to that city sent her heart lurching. There were so many memories there. But she couldn't hide from them forever. Maybe if she faced them she would be able to put them to rest. Winston obviously thought he was doing her a favor by offering her the trip. She couldn't refuse without hurting his feelings, so she smiled and nodded.

"I'd be happy to go," she replied.

"Good." He seemed pleased. "You'll enjoy Paris. You must take a few extra days and do some sightseeing while you're there. You've never been before, have you?" he asked suddenly, as if the possibility had just occurred to him.

"Once. But I really didn't see much. I was there on...other business."

"Well, you must see some sights this time. Ann will make all the arrangements for you. Is next week too soon?"

"No. That will be fine."

A few days later Ann presented her with her tickets, hotel confirmation, and a cash advance as she was preparing to leave work.

"I've checked everything, and it's all in order," Ann told her.

"Good. I won't even bother to look, then. I need every minute I have to finish up a few things here."

Just then Winston poked his head out of his office. "Just wanted to tell you to have a good trip," he said cheerily. "Are you taking some extra time?"

"Yes. That was an offer I couldn't refuse." What she didn't tell him was that she intended to spend those extra days sightseeing in England.

"Good, good. You'll enjoy Paris. Well, have a nice time."

It wasn't until she got into the cab at the airport in Paris that Brooke checked for the address of her hotel. At the sight of the name printed on the confirmation slip she caught her breath. She'd never even considered the possibility that the museum would book her into Alan's hotel! Winston had enclosed a note with the hotel confirmation, and her eyes quickly scanned it.

"This is a bit nicer than most of the places we stay when traveling on business, but you deserve a treat. I

172

stayed there once a few years ago and it is elegant. Enjoy."

Brooke closed her eyes. There was no way she could stay at Alan's hotel.

"Mademoiselle? I need the address, please."

Brooke opened her eyes and stared at the cab driver.

"I wonder...could you possibly recommend a good hotel? I...I've changed my mind about where I want to stay."

"It is so late in the day," he said, shaking his head. "And this is such a busy season. If you have a reservation, I think you should use it, mademoiselle. We could look, but..." He raised his hands and shrugged discouragingly.

Brooke frowned and looked down at the slip of paper in her hand. *Be logical*, she told herself sternly. The chances of meeting Alan were slim. He had his own apartment when he was in the city—which was only a small percentage of the time. And she would be there less than twenty-four hours. It was highly unlikely that they would meet.

"All right. I'll stay here." Brooke gave the cab driver the address and leaned back. It was actually rather funny, the way fate had conspired against her. *Maybe someday I'll be able to laugh about it*, she thought ruefully.

The drive to the hotel was all too short, and soon they pulled up in front of the familiar yellow and white striped canopy. A smartly dressed doorman opened the door, and while she settled her bill with the driver, her luggage—one small suitcase—was removed from the front seat.

"Welcome, mademoiselle," the doorman smiled at her as he opened the door to admit her to the elegantly furnished lobby she remembered so well. Alan had given her a tour during their stay in Paris, and it was just as it had been the last time she'd seen it. A quick glance around told her that he was not there, and she gave a sigh of relief.

None of the staff recognized her, although she thought someone might. The only bad moment came when her registration was pulled. The clerk frowned for a moment as he stared at the piece of paper.

"Brooke Peyton. A most unusual name, mademoiselle, yet familiar. Have you visited us before?"

"No," she said quickly in alarm, and then forced herself to smile. "Perhaps you've had another guest with a similar name."

"Perhaps," he shrugged, smiling. "You will be in room 405. Just let me know if you need anything."

"Thank you. I will."

Once in her room, Brooke allowed herself only a few minutes to admire the rich, deep blue furnishings. Then she placed a call to the antique dealer to let him know that she'd arrived and to confirm her appointment for early the next morning. That would give her plenty of time to catch her late-afternoon flight. She laid out her clothes for the next day, glancing at her watch as she did so. It was time for dinner, and all she had eaten so far that day was a snack on the plane. The cab had passed a small cafe about a block from the hotel, and rather than risk being recognized in the hotel she decided to walk to the cafe and get a sandwich.

She brushed her hair quickly and slipped into a trench coat and comfortable shoes. Not exactly the height of fashion, she thought wryly, but appropriate for her lifestyle now. The last time she'd been here she'd worn a beautiful designer gown, and she and Alan had been on their way to dinner and a show. She had felt lovely that night and had basked in the warm glow radiating from Alan's eyes.

Brooke was so lost in reminiscences that she didn't realize the elevator had arrived until the door started to slide open. She prepared to step inside and then froze, one hand at her throat and the other on the edge of the elevator. Alan and Monique were standing inside. She felt the blood drain from her face, and her eyes locked with Alan's.

He returned her stare, and his face seemed as tense and shocked as her own. The elevator door started to close and Brooke quickly stepped back. As if recovering from a trance, Alan leaned forward and pressed the "door open" button.

Monique was the first to fully recover, and as Alan pressed the button she smiled—a smile that didn't quite reach her eyes.

"Why, Brooke! What a surprise! Are you going down?" Numbly, Brooke nodded. "Well, there's plenty of room." Monique stepped closer to Alan and tucked her arm in his.

Brooke was left with no choice but to join them. Alan was wearing a tuxedo and Monique was dressed in a stunning royal blue evening gown. Brooke felt colorless and shabby beside her.

"Well, Brooke, what brings you here?" Monique asked brightly. The question was posed conversationally, but Brooke detected an undertone of intense interest.

"I'm here on business," Brooke replied shortly.

Alan had remained silent during this exchange, but now he turned to her and fixed the intense gray eyes she remembered so well on her.

"How long will you be in town?"

"Just until tomorrow."

"Oh, what a shame!" Monique gushed, but Brooke heard the relief in her voice. "Paris should be savored slowly. Whenever Alan and I come, we like to take our time and enjoy the city, don't we, dear?" She turned and gave him an intimate smile.

Alan, however, seemed oblivious to her insinuation. He just continued to stare at Brooke.

Brooke shifted uncomfortably under his gaze. Her whole body was trembling, and as soon as the elevator door opened she stepped outside. Monique and Alan followed her.

"Well, you must enjoy your stay, even if it is a short one," Monique told her.

"Thank you," Brooke replied stiffly.

"Will you be coming again soon?"

"I doubt it." She saw Monique smile with satisfaction at her response.

"Well, Alan, dear, we'll be late for the reception if we don't hurry. And you know I don't like to be too late. Fashionably late, yes, but not too late." She gave a brittle laugh and then turned to Brooke. "Such a pleasure seeing you, Brooke. You will forgive us if we run, won't you?" Without waiting for her to reply, Monique turned her attention back to Alan. "Shall we go?"

"Yes." He seemed to be still visibly shaken by the encounter. That was apparent even to Brooke, who was also in the same unsettled state. "Can we drop you off somewhere?" he offered.

"No thanks. I'm just going around the corner to get a bite to eat."

"Well, have a nice evening," Monique said, and taking Alan's arm, she physically turned him away from Brooke. Brooke heard her high-pitched laughter as they hurried across the lobby.

She was seated in the restaurant staring at the menu before she became fully aware of her surroundings. She didn't even remember walking to the cafe. Her mind had been whirling, and only now was she able to organize her thoughts.

There was only one thing she could do. She'd get up early tomorrow and check out before she went to visit the antique dealer. Then she wouldn't have to come back to the hotel. And she'd be gone long before Alan got up. Judging by his attire, it would be a late night for him, and he probably would want to sleep longer than usual.

Brooke tried desperately to quell the longing for

him that had resurfaced the moment she'd seen him. It was as if they'd never been apart. The second their eyes met, she'd wanted him to take her in his arms and hold her, but instead she'd been forced to stand there in agony while Monique made it clear that his arms now belonged to her.

With a deep, shuddering sigh, Brooke pushed her food away. Brooding over the situation wouldn't help. The best thing to do was to try and forget it and move forward instead of looking back.

Despite her resolve, Brooke spent an almost sleepless night tossing and turning. She wanted to be sure she was up and away long before Alan awoke. She'd survived one encounter, but she wasn't about to risk another.

Finally, as the sun was just beginning to cast its pale morning light, Brooke rose, dressed, and gathered her things together. The halls of the hotel were silent at that early hour, and even the lobby was practically deserted. The desk was manned only by a young clerk who smiled as she approached.

"Bonjour, mademoiselle. You are getting an early start."

"I have a lot of things to do today," she said, smiling.

"Then I will prepare your bill quickly. Was everything satisfactory?"

"Yes. Everything was fine."

"Très bien. If I may have the key, I will have your bill ready in just a moment." Brooke handed him the key and he selected a sheet from the file, scanning it quickly. He looked up and smiled. "It will be just a moment, mademoiselle. If you will excuse me?" He disappeared through a door behind the desk.

Brooke glanced around the lobby once more, noting again the tasteful furnishings—bowls of fresh flowers, ornate chandeliers, thick carpets, and richly upholstered furniture. It was a quietly elegant hotel, perfect in every respect.

Brooke turned back to the desk, aware that the clerk had been gone an inordinately long time. What was keeping him? She glanced at her watch, and then looked around the desk in vain for a bell or buzzer of some sort. Could the man have forgotten her? If he didn't come soon she would have—

"Good morning, Brooke. Leaving so soon?"

## Chapter Fifteen

Brooke's heart flew to her throat at the sound of the familiar voice, and slowly she turned to face Alan, who was strolling toward her across the lobby, his hands in the pockets of his slacks.

"How...how did you know I was leaving?" she faltered.

"I have very good employees. They follow my instructions to the letter."

"Oh." So he had warned the clerk to tip him off when she checked out. But why?

"It's a bit early to be leaving, isn't it?" he asked. He leaned casually against the counter, arms folded across his chest.

"I have a lot to do today. I didn't see any reason to come back to the hotel after my appointment." She reached down and picked up her suitcase. "I...I'm going to be late. Would you just...just send the bill to the museum, please? The address is on the reservation slip." She moved away but he took her arm in a steel grip and turned her to face him. Gone was the studied casualness, and his voice was determined when he spoke.

"I let you walk away once, Brooke. I'm not going to make the same mistake again."

Brooke made an effort to free herself from his grip,

179

but his hand tightened. "Alan, please let me go. We have nothing to discuss."

"I think we do. And until we do, you're not leaving."

"I have an appointment. In less than half an hour. I have to keep it," she pleaded. "My boss trusts me to carry out this assignment and I don't want to disappoint him."

A shadow crossed his face, and Brooke pressed her advantage. "I have to go, Alan," she insisted more firmly.

"All right." But he didn't let go of her arm. Instead, before she realized what he was doing, with his free hand he took her suitcase. She looked at him in surprise. "But this is staying here. And I want your promise that you'll come back here to pick it up before you leave. We are going to talk, one way or the other. Either now or later."

Brooke sighed. Maybe he wanted to talk about the annulment. "Okay," she agreed. "I'll probably be back before noon. I'll tell the desk clerk when I return."

He nodded, satisfied, and dropped her arm. "Until later, then." He turned and walked back in the direction from which he'd come.

Brooke watched him go and then drew a shaky breath. The desk clerk had quietly reappeared and was now stowing her suitcase behind the desk. So the hotel was efficient after all, she thought wryly.

Brooke took care of her business quickly. The artifact was in good shape, and she supervised its careful packing, clutching it gingerly as she left the shop. Winston would be pleased, she knew. It was exactly what they'd been looking for to complete the exhibit.

As she had promised, Brooke stopped at the desk on her return.

"Ah, oui, Mademoiselle Peyton. Monsieur d'Aprix asked that I give you this." The clerk handed her an envelope. "And your suitcase has been returned to your room."

"Thank you." She took it and made her way toward the elevator. She slit the envelope and quickly scanned the few written lines.

I'll meet you in the lobby at 1:00 and we'll go somewhere for lunch. Alan.

Brooke breathed a sigh of relief and glanced at her watch. That gave her an hour and a half. Although she told herself to stay calm, she could not stop her heart from beating rapidly and her hands from trembling. Despite herself, she wanted to have this time alone with Alan.

She searched through her suitcase in disgust. She'd packed for business, not pleasure, and the only dress she'd brought was a simple lavender silk shirtwaist, one of the outfits she'd acquired while on the Riviera. It wasn't fancy, but it did look good on her. It was open at the neck and revealed the delicate ivory of her skin.

Brooke donned the dress, pausing for a moment to open the small locket on the slender gold chain which still hung around her neck. She had worn it almost constantly since she'd bought it, and she smiled a bit at her own sentimentality as she gazed at the dried rose petal from her wedding bouquet. Finally she closed it and set to work on her makeup and hair.

At last she was satisfied, and she stood back for one more look in the mirror. It was hard to believe that the woman staring back at her was the same person who'd set off for a carefree European adventure a few months ago. So much had happened since that time. Yet externally it was hard to tell that anything at all had occurred. She'd grown thinner, it was true, and there was a new depth and sadness to her eyes. But that, she was sure, was visible only to her.

A glance at her watch told her it was time to go to the lobby, and she tried to slow the staccato beat of her heart by pausing a moment to take a few deep breaths. She felt more nervous about this meeting than she had about any other in her life.

Alan was waiting for her when she entered the lobby, and his frown changed to a look of relief when he caught sight of her. "I was afraid you might not come," he told her when she was within speaking distance.

"I always keep my promises," she said.

"Yes, I know." He said it softly, almost to himself. and Brooke looked at him questioningly. But he apparently didn't intend to explain that statement.

"I have a five o'clock flight, Alan, so..."

"We need to get started," he finished for her. She nodded.

"Can't we just talk here?" she suggested.

"No privacy," he shook his head. "But there's a secluded spot nearby." He took her arm and led her toward the door, and she followed unprotestingly. It was so nice to feel his arm on hers again!

He didn't speak at all as they walked the half-block to the restaurant, and Brooke followed his lead. She felt content just to be with him. She had missed him terribly, but she hadn't fully realized the depth of her loss until now, when she was back in his presence again.

They were seated in the tiny, quiet restaurant, removed both from the sight and sound of the busy street outside, and Alan had given their order to the waiter before he turned the discussion to personal matters.

"I know you're wondering why I asked you to see me today," he began slowly, as if feeling his way. He paused and looked at her, but she lowered her eyes, afraid that if she returned his look he would read the longing in them. "I was…surprised to see you yesterday," he continued.

"I was surprised to see you, too. I didn't even know I was staying in your hotel until I got to Paris," she said. *What an inane remark*! And *surprised* wasn't the right word, anyway. *Shocked. Startled. Jolted.* They were much more accurate.

"Why didn't you accept the checks I sent you?" he asked suddenly.

She stared at him, taken aback by his unexpected question. She played with the gold chain and locket around her neck as she tried to think up a suitable answer.

"I…I didn't need the money. I have a job. Anyway, I was glad to do a favor for you, after all you did for me."

He watched her speculatively in silence.

"That's a pretty locket. May I?" Before she had time to protest he had taken it in his hand and flipped it open. These rapid changes in subject matter were confusing her, and when he raised his eyes to hers questioningly at the contents of the locket, she grew even more flustered.

"A dried flower petal? How long have you had this, Brooke?"

"Since our wedding," she replied, unable to think up a plausible lie in her confused state. "Just sentimental, I guess." She tried to pass it off lightly. "A woman doesn't get married that often."

Silently he let go of the locket, and she put it back inside the neck of her dress—where it should have been all along. She was angry with herself for wearing it. She just wasn't thinking straight.

Alan remained silent for a few more moments, but at last he spoke. "You know, Brooke, I discovered something yesterday." He looked down at the table and toyed with his glass. It was almost as if he were thinking out loud. "I really thought I had gotten over you. I found out I was wrong. I discovered that since you left

183

I haven't been living—I've only been existing. It took the shock of seeing you again to make me realize that."

Brooke stared at him. Were her ears playing tricks on her? "I...I don't understand," she said breathlessly.

He looked at her and gave a wry smile. "I'm not being very articulate, am I? Well, let me try again. That day you left, months ago, you took me off guard. You didn't give me a chance to say the things I wanted to say. I'd like to say them now."

"But Alan," she protested, "I stayed as long as you needed me. My usefulness was finished, wasn't it?"

"Actually, my dear, I was hoping it was just beginning," he replied softly as he took her cold hand in a warm clasp across the table. Brooke's heart jumped to her throat at his tone and touch.

"What do you mean?" she whispered, almost afraid to ask, yet unable to stop the hope that was rising within her.

"Why do you think I never sent the annulment papers?"

"I...I don't know."

"Why didn't you ask about them?"

"There was no one else," she shrugged. "It didn't matter. But I was surprised that you didn't send them," she admitted. "I thought you'd be anxious to be free of me so you could marry Monique." The words were out before she could stop them.

"Monique?"

"Well, I saw your picture with her in one of those gossip sheets, so—"

"Brooke!" he admonished her with mock sternness. "You don't read those things, do you?"

"Not usually," she defended herself. "But anyway, Monique said..." Brooke stopped. There was no sense going over all this, opening old wounds.

"Go on," Alan demanded, a frown darkening his face. "What else did Monique say?"

"It's not important."

184

"It is to me."

He had that imperious note in his voice, and with a sigh Brooke relented. "Well, she hinted that you two were to be married eventually." Brooke tried to keep her voice casual, but even now it hurt to say those words. "And she said that I wouldn't fit into your lifestyle—that I'd be more of a hindrance than a help, and that you'd get tired of me." Hard as she tried, she couldn't keep the hurt out of her voice, and she lowered her eyes.

Alan reached across the table and lifted her chin gently with his fingers. "Brooke, Monique was never more than an acquaintance, a handy companion for social functions. Her intentions may have been more serious, but I made mine clear from the start. They were purely social—not romantic. You do believe that, don't you?"

Brooke nodded. She couldn't doubt the sincerity in his tone or the honesty in his eyes. She wanted to believe it.

"And as for growing tired of you—that would be impossible, Brooke. You have more depth of character and love of life than any woman I've ever met." He paused for a moment and when he continued his voice was more serious than Brooke had ever heard it. "I'd like you to come back, Brooke. As my wife. This time in the fullest sense of the word."

"Why?" she whispered.

"Oh Brooke, do you have to ask?" he said hoarsely, and the sudden rough tenderness in his tone told her all she needed to know.

"Alan, I waited so long..." Her voice was choked with emotion and a tear fell unchecked onto the snowy linen tablecloth, leaving a damp, dark patch. He looked at her, and the joy in his eyes was unmistakable.

"Why didn't you say something sooner?" he asked.

"I...I didn't think you loved me. And I was afraid if I

185

said anything you'd just feel sorry for me," she explained in a broken voice.

"Sorry for you? No, my feelings were much stronger than that," he told her with a soft laugh. "At first, after the accident, I felt a sense of responsibility, and that's why I offered you a place to stay while you recuperated. But as I got to know you I quickly realized how very special you are."

"Why didn't you tell me?"

"I had no idea you felt the same way. But I hoped that in time you would come to love me as much as I loved you." He squeezed her hand and smiled. "The only way I could think to keep you with me long enough for that love to have a chance to develop was to ask you to marry me."

"But I thought you just needed me to help you close that business deal with Nick," she said in confusion.

"I must admit that I misled you there," he smiled. "I hope you can forgive me. I just loved you so much that I was desperate."

Brooke glowed in the warmth of his words, but there were still some things that she didn't understand.

"Alan, if you loved me, why did you treat me so coldly after...that night in Paris?"

"It was because I loved you so much that I treated you that way," he said fervently. "I wanted you more than I can say. Do you have any idea how difficult it was for me to lie in that bed night after night alone, when you were so close? It took all my will power not to open that connecting door. But I thought I needed to give you time to want me. I was afraid after that night in Paris that I'd ruined my chances. I was so afraid you'd leave, and I wouldn't have blamed you if you had.

"When you decided to stay, the only way I could think to avoid repeating the scene was to stay as aloof as possible. You'll never know how hard it was to be so close to you and not to be able to touch you and tell you how much I loved you. Sometimes I thought I couldn't bear it. I wanted you so much!

"And that day you had lunch with the sailor I lost my head completely. I thought maybe you were in love with him."

"I think I have some idea of how you felt, Alan," Brooke smiled, remembering her own feelings about Monique.

"There's one thing more I want you to understand, Brooke," Alan added. "I know I have a reputation as a playboy. That's because I'm wealthy, single, and socially prominent. The reputation comes with the territory. But I'm not like that. You're the only woman I've ever cared about deeply. I value love and commitment too much to treat it as lightly as my reputation leads people to believe."

She took his hand across the table and smiled tenderly into his eyes. "You didn't have to tell me that, Alan. I knew it—from the first when you told me about your parents. I never questioned your integrity. I couldn't have loved you if I had."

She paused and smiled into Alan's eyes.

"You know, I think Mrs. Bates would have been pleased with the way things turned out for us. She believed that *love* was the most wonderful gift of all, so it seems fitting that our love was a result of her legacy to me. Without her generosity, I would never have met you—or fallen in love with you."

She reached over and took Alan's hand. "I just can't believe this is really happening," she said a moment later, her love openly reflected in her eyes. "I think you'd better pinch me, Alan."

"I'll do better than that," he said in return, and leaning across the table he pulled her close, his warm lips resting on hers in a lingering kiss. She responded with all the longing that had been building inside her for months, and they were alone in a world without time.

At last Brooke pulled away and lowered her eyes. "Alan, there are people here," she protested halfheartedly.

"This is a very intimate place, and it's not that crowded," he said softly, his lips close to her ear. He started to reach for her again, but she drew away.

"What about my plane?"

In response he pulled her close again. "We've wasted enough time as it is, Brooke," he whispered as his lips brushed her forehead. "Are you going to let a plane interfere?"

She reached for him, her eyes glowing with passion.

"What plane?" she murmured as his lips claimed hers.

## About the Author

A communications manager and executive speech writer for a Fortune 500 company by day and a romance writer by night, Irene Hannon has had a lifelong love affair with words. She also enjoys singing, and in her "spare" time performs in community musical theatre productions. Irene and her husband, Tom, live in their native Missouri.

Forever Romances are inspirational romances designed to bring you a joyful, heart-lifting reading experience. If you would like more information about joining our Forever Romance book series, please write to us:

Guideposts Customer Service
39 Seminary Hill Road
Carmel, NY 10512

Forever Romances are chosen by the same staff that prepares *Guideposts*, a monthly magazine filled with true stories of people's adventures in faith. *Guideposts* is not sold on the newsstand. It's available by subscription only. And subscribing is easy. Write to the address above and you can begin reading *Guideposts* soon. When you subscribe, each month you can count on receiving exciting new evidence of God's Presence, His Guidance and His limitless love for all of us.